Talon's Grip

A Novel By

Russ Hall

Rival Media
PUBLISHING

This is a work of fiction. Names, characters, places and incidents are either the products of the author's imagination or are used fictitiously, and any resemblance to actual persons, living or dead, events, or locales is entirely coincidental.

Copyright © Russ Hall 2009

Cover created by:

Sean M. Smith, Rival Media, LLC

Published in 2009 by:
Rival Media Publishing
3100 Independence Pkwy, Suite 311, #368
Plano, Texas 75075
rivalmediapub.com

Talon's Grip
ISBN – 13: 978-0-578-04010-3

Library of Congress Catalog Card Number pending

Chapter One

Look through any crowd of people and some individuals stand out. They sparkle. But for each of these individuals, there were others you have a hard time noticing at all. They are the ones who interested Arthur Sanderson, the invisible ones. He wanted to understand them, to be more like them.

An airport crowd is full of people who, by background or bearing, have learned to be as drab and unnoticeable as possible. They slink to the corners, lean on the walls, avoid eye contact, and huddle in the rows of seats. Their ability to blend in with their surroundings is an art form. What better place to study their styles and manners than in the hubbub of people pulsing in waves to and from gates, pouring out of jet bridge doorways to rush toward restrooms, or to surge through the terminal toward the baggage area an escalator flight down after passing through the security gate.

That regular hum of activity stopped at the first gunshot.

The blast of that shot set off a half-a-clip answering burst from an automatic weapon, the bullets ricocheting high off the walls. Glass shattered. Screams mingled in the uproar and people dove to the floor all around Arthur. He dropped to the floor against a support pillar and slid lower down the side of it, out of the way of people who ran—one shoved aside a wheelchair, and some even knocked down hysterical children. If you want chaos with spurs, try having someone spray an Uzi about inside an airport terminal.

In seconds every person crouched or lay on the floor. Screams mingled with moans. The sound of harsh heels clicked in a run that came hard and fast down the hallway. The man out in front held a pistol and looked back over his shoulder. He ran in steps that made no sound. The clicking heel steps came from the second man, the one with the automatic in his hand.

A nearly invisible man Arthur had watched earlier lounge against the wall between a newsstand and a yogurt shop drew a black pistol out from his nylon wind jacket. He had sure looked drab and unnoticeable before in his worn sneakers and rumpled khaki slacks. Try to ignore him now.

The running man's face turned toward Arthur. It was a face he had not seen in forty years, Frankie Lane, a high school classmate of his. They had been friends for a while, and then they had not.

"Hey," Arthur yelled, and pointed toward the man drawing his gun.

Frankie glanced that way, and without pause fired a shot that slammed the guy back into the wall.

The automatic weapon behind him lit up again and Frankie dove, sliding across the polished tile right at Arthur. His gun skittered loose from his hand and slid separately until it came to rest against Arthur's thigh. Frankie's face turned toward Arthur, not in panic, or fear, but as if considering him. The whole moment seemed to reel by in extreme slow motion. Arthur saw the standing man with the automatic slow down and point it.

In life there come moments when, if time could stop, you would deliberate and decide, choose better than you do. But the moment doesn't stop, and you have to choose in a split second, a life-changing shift that sends you reeling off in a new direction, one from which you can never return.

There was no time to reminisce about Frankie, or make amends about anything he might have done different in the past. Arthur knew him, though, and didn't know the ones chasing him and shooting at him. He picked up the gun, aimed it at the man with the automatic, and squeezed the trigger.

The Uzi clattered to the floor as the man flew backward. Frankie jumped up, yanked Arthur to his feet, switched the gun from Arthur's to his own hand, and whisked them around and over the people huddled on the ground, many who still covered their heads. Frankie led the way, not back toward the security gates and escalator to the baggage area but to a door beside the nearest jet bridge. A large sign on it proclaimed:

> # Stop
>
> Entering SIDA Area
> Airport I.D. Required
> No Piggybacking
> Secure Door Upon Entering
> Report Suspicious Activity

Arthur glanced back. The usual frenzy of the airport had erupted into a higher level of mayhem than he could have imagined possible. A couple of uniformed security officers tried to push through the crowd of hysterical people who had struggled back to their feet and now rushed in a mass of screams and pushing toward the main exit. He turned back in time to see Frankie swipe a card and open the door. Frankie tugged him through and a cool breeze swept across them. They clattered down steel stairs. Arthur suspected his eyes looked like a frightened rabbit pulled out of its hole. What had he done? Only a few times in his life had he ever pulled a trigger, and now he had killed a man. With only those few seconds to respond he had taken action to save someone he knew. He knew nothing about Frankie. Was he a good guy, or some escaping menace? In the course of playing and replaying the scene in his head, Arthur pictured the man with the automatic. He had been going to shoot, no matter what. That was not the way of law enforcement, and that was what, in a bare split second, had decided and swayed him. Yet he had shot a man dead. His head struggled to wrap around that, at the same time sweeping the area around them to see if they had been spotted.

In spite of the noise and ruckus inside, the activity around the planes at the gates still seemed normal. Fuel trucks pulled up, smaller carts towed baggage wagons to waiting luggage compartments, and men and women in airport coveralls found time to huddle and chat in small circles. Planes lifted off the ground and swooped down to land in their routine patterns in a sky where the clouds looked edged in purple and beams of sunlight burst out in many directions like yellow spears, all very Salvador Dali to Arthur's jangled state of mind. He would not have been surprised to see a drooping clock hanging from the side of one of the clouds.

They slid along a wall and Frankie tugged him into a room filled with lockers. Arthur watched the door, expecting any moment to see men with guns burst through. Frankie handed him a set of the blue coveralls like some of the ground crew wore. "Here, put this on."

Frankie got his on quickly enough, and tugged on knee pads and a headset meant to protect the ears against noise. By the time Arthur had struggled into his outfit, Frankie had clipboards for them and handed him one. "Come on."

A loud siren began to sound. Arthur wrestled with whether he was doing the right thing, whether he should stay and face up to any consequences. He had so little an idea of what was going on, he stayed mute and followed

Frankie.

"Do you have a car?"

He nodded, realized Frankie had not looked back, so he said, "Yes. In P-five. The long-term parking garage."

Cars and people hurried in an uncertain tangle toward the exit as Frankie, with Arthur close behind, wove through the cars in short-term parking. They might have been detained then if it had not been for the gear they wore. Arthur pointed the way to his car with a hand that trembled like an aspen leaf in a gusting breeze. At his three-year old Land Rover, Frankie held out a hand for the keys and Arthur handed them to him. Frankie tugged off his coveralls and tossed them, the clipboard and the ear covers into the back seat before he slid into the driver's side. Arthur caught himself before he asked, realized airport employees would leave by another exit, and took off the coveralls he wore.

No one had told the attendants at the parking lot pay booths what to do yet, so the Rover spiraled down the exit ramp and they waited through a short line. Arthur breathed in short gulps all the while, then dug out his wallet and paid for the short stay, and they were soon on the road that led away from the airport toward Columbus. He glanced back. The sun still struggled to send light through the tangled mat of clouds that now seemed a somber and sad gray. The chaos at the terminal faded into the distance behind them. Blue and red lights flashed at every corner of the central cluster of buildings. He turned to look ahead. In the oncoming lanes vehicles with lights and sirens going, ambulances, police cars, and a black SWAT truck among them, rushed toward the airport. Traffic on that side pulled over to let them by. Arthur took the first deep breath he had drawn in a while.

Frankie turned on the radio and went from station to station until he got the news he was after. The airport had closed down, the terminal had been sealed, and no more cars were being allowed out of the parking area. There was something about a sky marshal and a federal officer. He clicked the radio off.

"Don't think for a minute we weren't lucky back there," Frankie said, his eyes intent on the traffic ahead.

Arthur fingered the sleeve of his brown tweed sports jacket he had torn without noticing during their escape. "Yeah, lucky," he said, not surprised at a quaver in his voice. "I get the feeling you're a regular lucky kind of guy these days, Frankie."

"Frankie. I haven't heard that in many a moon." The corner of his mouth tugged up for a second. "I suspect you're trying to sort out whether I'm one of the good guys or not."

He had hit precisely on what noodled around in Arthur's still-shaken brain.

"It depends on your point of view," he said, not helping Arthur's confusion.

An instant-long flashback of the man he had shot flying through the air swept over him and a wave of nausea shot up from his ankles to punch him in the stomach. His hand shot up to his mouth and he gagged.

"Don't you hurl out the window. They'll see that. Do it

on the floor," Frankie snapped.

Arthur forced himself to swallow back the tangy harsh taste of bile. He rubbed the moist corner of one eye. Shudders ran up and down his limbs. He didn't feel any better. *Be strong.* He sought to be far calmer than he looked, tried to cross his legs. When that didn't work he just sat still.

Frankie kept quiet as he took the 270 loop around the city and turned onto a road Arthur recognized. Without asking his address, Frankie headed toward where Arthur lived, in the area where they had both grown up.

Arthur saw him glance his way a couple of times to take in the white temples and gray hairs speckled in Arthur's hair as well as checking to see that his hands still shook. Though the same age, Frankie's hair was darker, and he seemed far calmer. Forty years. It was a long time.

"This the first time you ever shot anyone?" Frankie said after they passed through the outskirts of Columbus and traffic thinned out on the four-lane highway.

"Yes, and the last, I hope."

"Well, thanks. You losing your cherry on that came at a good time—for me."

Arthur still dealt with a heartbeat that felt like Saturday at the races. It had been a traumatic day—one minute calm and the next shaken not stirred. Frankie sure looked different from the boy he had gone to school with. Frankie's high school face had been rounded, with blurred lines, and a weak mouth. This one was nothing like it, although it was him all right. The face Arthur looked at now had seen a lot of cruel and heartless things and had survived twenty years past flinching at any of it. The younger Frankie may not have been fat, but he was soft, and far from fit back then. This version, Arthur's age, looked lithe, quick, hard, and alert. Extensive physical training had helped the years hone him firm. Arthur was the one with a few extra pounds now. They had somehow traded places through the years.

"What *do* people call you these days?" Arthur asked.

"Frank will do just fine," he said, rolling the name on his tongue as if regaining the familiar feel of it.

"Look, pull over, Frank," Arthur said. "We need to talk. I mean it. Pull the hell over, dammit."

He gave Arthur a quick glance and kept going.

"I don't suppose you're going to tell me what that was all about."

"Wish I could," he said. "But you know how that is."

"No. No, I don't. It's not one of those things where you'd have to kill me if you say, is it?"

Frankie glanced at him. "See. You're getting your humor back. That's a good sign."

Arthur looked out his side window, said nothing.

"You still as shy as you were? Or have you gotten worse?"

Arthur's lips stayed pressed tight for a few more miles. "What have you gotten me into, Frank? Can you tell me that?"

"If I could erase the past few minutes and leave things as they were before you saw me, don't you think I'd do that?"

"You still haven't answered the question."

"Before you get yourself worked up into a self-righteous frenzy, why don't you feel around and see if you're injured or shot. A lot of people in a situation like that would have come out a whole lot worse."

Arthur blinked and looked away. The familiar scenery of fields and farms that peeled by past the window should have comforted him but failed to help with the surreal feeling that he might as well be taking steps on the moon. Life until the past few moments had a dull, cozy side to it that had just been rattled to the core. His mind raced through a lot that probably didn't matter. He had thought until a few moments ago that it was hard, impossible, to get a gun past airport security. But Frankie had managed somehow, and he was not alone.

"High school seems like about a million years ago, doesn't it?" Frankie said.

"I remember hazy bits of it."

"We were a ripe couple of geeks or nerds back then, weren't we."

"I do recall a time after I suggested we boycott prom and you argued in favor of going when you left me beside the road seven miles from town." Having touched on the moment Arthur could recall it as if it had just occurred—Frankie pulling over to the side of the road and ordering him out of the car. He had smoldered all the way back into town, and had not spoken to Frankie for the rest of their senior year. For that matter, Frankie had not spoken to him, either.

"You called me a name," Frankie said.

"*Obese el legardo*, I believe. It wasn't even good Spanish." Years later, there were times Arthur saw Frankie's side of it. Arthur had been no linguist and more of a jerk too than he liked to recall.

"Doesn't seem like such a big thing now, does it?" Frankie glanced his way. Arthur could not get over how lean and alert his face was, like a predator bird about to dive.

"Where have you been since high school?" Arthur said.

"Oh, here and there."

"Doing this and that, I suppose."

"Quite."

It felt maddening, expecting any second to hear sirens turn on behind them and pull them over. Frankie's stone cold calm only made Arthur's insides tossed all the more in lurching waves.

"Is there any way the authorities can connect any of this to me?" Arthur said.

"You did pull the trigger. There will be the usual check on which passengers didn't get on their planes. You might have left prints on the floor tiles for all you know. They'll have a record of who left the parking area as well."

"You're saying there's a pretty good chance?"

"It's a matter of time," Frankie said.

If Frankie had stopped the car and punched Arthur in the stomach with as much force as he could muster Arthur doubted if he could have stunned him more. In the opposing lanes a pair of state trooper cars raced by, their lights and sirens going, headed for the big city.

"Where are we going?" Arthur asked.

"Your place, for now. It's all we have. Do you have family, a wife and kids to think about?" He looked full at Arthur.

"No." Nor did Arthur have a dog, any kind of pet, or even a living plant. Is it really living if you are connected to nothing at all? Well, Arthur was sure connected now, whether he liked it or not.

"You're lucky then." Frankie's eyes swung back to the road.

"Yeah lucky," Arthur said.

Chapter Two

Frankie turned off the highway and steered down the county road where Arthur pointed. A short lane led to a sturdy stone gateway with a steel-barred gate. Ten-foot high deer fence ran off in both directions from the gate into thick-wooded hills.

"Whew," Frankie let out an impressed whistle. "I forgot I heard you'd bought the old Coxwell place."

"It's *my* place now." Arthur hit the button on the control that started the gate open.

"It's over a hundred acres, isn't it?"

It was bigger than that. Arthur had picked up a few other parcels that made it two hundred acres, which is a goodish-sized property in this part of the state. He felt in no mood to discuss real estate.

Spring was coming to the wooded ground around them. Clumps of mayapples and bloodroot formed green spots in the valleys and hillsides while redbud trees made bright purplish color splashes here and there among the budding trees not yet covered with leaves.

Through his partially open window the fecund odor of the woods swept in. It smelled of damp, dark soil, rich in decomposing leaves and bark, with a hint of earthworm and the green chlorophyll of young plants bursting upward.

Soon it would be the time of year he tromped through the woods searching for morels, with their spongy mushroom shape fixed in his mind. It was enough to make anyone feel at one with the earth. All great wines show the characteristics of the soil, and each of us, he knew, bears the earthy mark of where we have lived our lives. The spring smell of an Ohio woods usually resonated with everything that kept Arthur going. At the moment it made him want to vomit.

The drive wove up a hill and there was the house. Not much to look at from outside—a ranch-style three bedroom home with chipped brown paint. He opened the garage door with another button, and Frankie pulled the vehicle in, and turned off the engine.

Frankie didn't say anything until they were inside, then Arthur heard him take in a breath. Arthur had spent some time, and money, getting the inside the way he liked. The walls were paneled with dark wood, with hunter green trim on the crown molding; a breakfast nook's table and the kitchen countertop reflected the sheen of black granite. A wine rack and leaded-glass crystal stemware hung upside down ran along the wall, with a matched set of polished copper cookware over the range. The floors were hardwood with Persian rugs and the chairs and sofa were burgundy leather. The inside of the house had nothing to do with the outside, and that was what Arthur had intended. Frankie was the first person to see the inside in quite a while.

"Did you win the lottery, or strike oil?" Frankie stood looking up at a framed oil painting. Then let his eyes sweep across the shelves of leather-bound books.

Arthur should have felt good, proud, but he didn't. A picture of the man who had held the Uzi flying backward in the air kept playing and replaying in his head. Frankie glanced around. "No television?"

"No. Sorry."

Frankie walked across to the stereo system beside the fireplace, swung the glass door open and flipped on the radio. A piece by Mendelssohn boomed out of the speakers. He spun the tuner dial until he found an all-talk news station.

They listened a minute or two until they could determine that the officials were still sorting out the mess back at the airport. Peaceful Ohio was in an uproar, was never going to be the same. Neither Frankie nor Arthur got mentioned. Frankie saw the look on his face and toggled off the power. It felt even quieter than before.

"You've got a nice place here," Frankie said.

"Gosh, thanks."

"What do you do these days?"

"You're the one I should be asking that. I have the feeling anything I say will be dull by comparison."

Frankie ignored that. "Do you have a passport? You might get that together with a small travel kit, any cash you can round up, in case we have to move fast."

"How much time do you think we have?"

"Not much."

Frank moved about, looking everything over with cold and deliberate eyes.

"What in the hell have you gotten me into here,

15

Frankie," Arthur shouted. "You've got to tell me."

"I don't have to tell you anything."

"I saved your life, and you're starting to make me regret that."

"The phone's right over there. Call the authorities, if you like."

"You know I can't do that until I know what I'm in the middle of." In spite of himself Arthur had dropped from a shout to a nearly sensible loud voice.

"Welcome to my world."

"You don't know what you're doing and you drag me in?" Arthur's eyes swept his living room, taking it all in as if it belonged to someone else. He felt a twinge of embarrassment at how orderly everything seemed.

"I didn't drag. You leaped. You're the one who pulled that trigger. I didn't ask you to."

"I was doing what I thought I had to."

"And you're living in the consequences of your actions. Like I said, welcome to my world."

"You know, I live alone because being around people too much, or at all sometimes, I feel uptight and rattled. I wish you could have a peek at my insides at the moment."

"Round up your stuff," Frankie repeated. "We may have to move fast."

Now it was "we." Arthur guessed Frankie was right. Without meaning to, he had somehow bound himself at the hip to Frankie, and that after not seeing so much as a glimpse of him in all these years.

He looked around to the rows of leather-bound books

unread and hours not spent yet. In addition to those walks in the woods, he had been looking forward to that first sip of wine by the fireplace when chilly weather came.

"It's natural enough to miss things before they're gone," Frankie said. He had been watching Arthur. "Before a woman ever leaves you, it's possible to miss her."

"Just shut up," Arthur snapped.

"Right. Don't consider me the voice of reason just now."

Arthur plopped into the leather wing chair, his favorite reading spot. He knew where he kept their senior class album and felt half tempted to go have a look at the Frankie he had known. There were a few faces he would prefer not to see. Rolly Stanton, for that punch in the eye, and, of course, Donnie Angel, who always made him think of that spider who said, "Where I walk the grass dies." He looked over the current Frankie, who could have fared far better against the likes of Rolly or Donnie than the Frankie of that day. "It's all very nice to wax philosophical. I doubt your life is about to change much from whatever it was. What were you, some sort of spook? Or did you work for the other side?"

Frankie's eyes narrowed. "I meant that about getting a kit ready to roll. I'm not sure it'll be safe to stay the night here."

Arthur pushed himself up from the chair, spun and went into the kitchen. He swung the pantry door open. Shelves of cans and stored food lined the shelves along one wall. The opposing wall was covered by floor-to-ceiling wine racks filled with dusty bottles of Bordeaux, Burgundy, and other red wines. He swept aside a rug with his foot and tugged at a trapdoor ring. Anyone who has ever experienced a house fire knows it would have been nice to think ahead and have in one place everything you wanted to run from the house with if the place was afire. Arthur opened the fireproof safe and tugged out a small leather duffel bag. He didn't need to look inside. It held his passport, a hundred and fifty thousand in cash, and the handful of items he would miss if the place was destroyed. The rest was in safety deposit boxes, although he had crossed federal lines today and he doubted if any of that would matter much.

"Did you ever marry?"

Arthur realized Frankie stood right behind him, looking over his shoulder down into the safe.

"No," Arthur said. "You?"

"I wondered how you managed a place like this on your own," Frankie waved a hand at the inside of the home.

Arthur decided that would be the last time he answered a personal question for a while.

"Any guns? Ammo?" Frankie asked as Arthur flipped the safe closed and stood up, sweeping the rug back over the trapdoor after he closed it. "Nine millimeter would be nice, if you have it."

Arthur gave Frankie an irritated glance, swept past him on his way to the bedroom. At the closet, he took out one of his smallest soft leather travel bags and began to pack. Frankie drifted into the room while he pulled clothes from drawers and the closet, folded them, and shoved them into the bag.

"Look, I understand you being a little miffed," Frankie said.

"You don't understand anything. Nor do I imagine you care about anything but yourself."

Frankie started to say something, then shrugged and turned to go out into the living room. When Arthur came out of the bedroom, Frankie had pulled aside one corner of the drawn picture window curtains and peeked outside.

"Anyone storming up the hill?" Arthur asked.

"Not yet."

"Just how much poison are you these days, Frankie?"

"It's not me. The world's gotten to be an ambiguous place." He dropped the curtain corner and turned to Arthur. "Look, if it makes you feel better I'm sorry you're in this mess. I'm used to getting along fine on my own. I was surprised as dammit to see you there at the airport when things went a little south. But it was no notion of mine to get you involved."

"A little south?" Arthur said. He dropped the two bags beside the wing chair and settled into it. He sought to calm his insides, which felt like a coffee percolator shifting into overdrive. Rage is one of the phases of mourning. Feathers of it tickled up and down his limbs, mixed with a stew of fear and uncertainty, all while he sought to seem calm. "We have a few moments. Why don't you catch me up on what you've been doing for the past few years? The last I recall hearing of you some guys after prom had dropped you off in front of your house with you too drunk on vodka and orange soda to crawl inside, though you had enough presence of mind to throw up on your dad's shoes."

"Kind of supports your decision not to attend prom, doesn't it?"

"The next I knew you'd enlisted. Those were tough times. Viet Nam. I'm surprised you made it back at all. We had a number of classmates who didn't."

"I guess you were off to graduate school, or something equally eggheaded."

That's exactly where Arthur had been, although there was no win-win in even nodding. He said nothing.

"That's you all over," Frankie said. "Always the world expert on everything, and with second-hand info at that, before you even have a chance to hear the whole story."

"I'm waiting. Tell away. There's nothing I'd like better than to know what you're up to."

It looked for a moment as if Frankie would answer. A crash interrupted. The curtains across the picture window jerked and a tear gas grenade rolled across the living room floor. A swirl of greenish-yellow smoke lifted from it. Frankie held a hand across his mouth and nose and ran toward the garage. Arthur grabbed his bags and did the best he could at imitating him, though his eyes squinted almost shut on their own and his nose felt like he breathed flames.

Chapter Three

This was no visit by the local police—no warning voices through bull horns or any of the usual niceties. Bullets slapped against the side of the house, some breaking through windows. One burst a Navaho vase on the fireplace mantel. A row of holes climbed across one wall and took out an oil painting and gave a bust of Mark Twain a third eye. Arthur and Frankie both crouched low on the floor and crawled as fast as they could go, staying as close to the hardwood floor as they could get without scraping up splinters. Frankie had his gun out and ready in one hand.

Arthur snatched glimpses of the house as bullets shredded it to bits. He felt each hit as a physical pain, though it would have been worse if the bullets were shredding him and not just everything he valued.

At the passageway to the garage he eased ahead to open the door and slip through, with Frankie close enough behind to be a second skin. Frankie hadn't asked where they were headed, which was to his credit. It wasn't a really good time for a chat.

The Land Rover tilted on one flat tire and the glass from a couple of its windows that had been knocked out were sprinkled in glittering bits across the floor. It was just as well the vehicle hadn't been part of what Arthur intended. As they crawled past the Rover a ricocheting bullet took out another of its tires and barely missed them. Instead it embedded in a can of paint that began to ooze into a pool of wet brown across the concrete behind them. Arthur had been meaning to paint the house. There was one chore he might get to skip.

He wriggled close along the base of a horizontal freezer and slipped under the workbench that ran along one side of the garage. He signaled to Frankie to stay down, then unlatched a low door and eased it open a fraction of an inch. He had made this small doorway to get the mower in and out of the garage without opening the big doors, though why he maintained a small lawn and garden out in the middle of the wilderness was less clear to him at the moment.

Timing meant everything. Feet pounded by just before he looked outside. The way ahead looked clear for the moment. A low culvert ran down along the inside of a hedge he had planted to hide repair work on a pipeline to the septic tank. The pump to a leach field was housed in a low wooden box ahead. A man in camouflage coveralls, holding what looked like a Mac 10, leaped up from behind the pump's box and without glancing Arthur's way ran around toward the front of the house.

For part of a second Arthur thought of rushing out and giving himself up. If they had been dressed in uniforms or looked anything like a SWAT team he might have. But their dress and professional manner confirmed that they had nothing to do with law enforcement as Arthur knew it. He still didn't know what sticky business Frankie was immersed in, and Arthur along with him, but they were up to their eyebrows against some very nasty looking and unhesitant shooters.

The thought motivated him as he burst out the spring-loaded door with Frankie close on his heels. They stayed low-to-the-ground and wriggled across the dirt staying as near to the hedge as they could. As soon as they got to the septic pump box the ground gave way to a downward tilted ravine filled with the beginnings of this year's berry patch. The sounds of shots being fired toward the house behind them heightened in intensity. Arthur didn't hesitate to surge down through the briars that snatched at his pant cuffs and tugged at the light leather jacket he had switched to before leaving.

A flurry of louder shouting made him think they had been spotted, which only made him scurry faster. It must have come from those goons kicking in the door. Only a few moments would pass before the uninvited guests discovered Arthur and Frankie had slipped away. Ahead, at the bottom of the ravine, a valley opened into a creek lined with a thicker growth of cottonwoods and shrubs. Arthur walked right into the stream and kept in it as he ran splashing up its ankle-deep flow as fast as he could. Muddy swirls marked where his feet had been, but they would soon disappear. Where he could he kept his steps on underwater gravel bars where the stones could fall back into place after their steps.

His breath came in short gasps. He didn't know when he had run faster. Bullets will do that.

"Where are you going?" Frankie whispered.

23

Arthur waved ahead and kept running. He didn't know if they had brought dogs, but going up the creek might throw off a foot chase. He had to hope.

Ahead he saw the first of the fence—his own ten-foot high deer fence. There was a low spot at the surface of the creek that dipped lower than the fence he had been meaning to fix to keep some of the critter traffic down. It was another chore he felt glad he had not gotten time to do. On the other side a culvert passed under the highway. They could hear the buzz of cars going by as they slipped under the fence, getting all the way wet as they did. Then they ran through the culvert and came out on the other side. Arthur bent and held his knees, gasping for breath.

"Come on," Frankie hissed. "No time for resting yet."

"I'm not resting," Arthur panted. "I'm keeping myself alive by breathing."

"Come on." Frankie struggled over a three-strand barbed-wire fence and took off in a run toward the thickest part of the woods on the other side. It had been let grow more wild than on Arthur's side. Spring mushrooms would be sprouting thick in the dead leaves and mulch of bark soon. He had scouted the area by sneaking through the fences before in this direction. This was not the time to dwell on activities like that. He pushed himself away from the concrete culvert wall and took off after Frankie, who was already almost to the thickest stand of trees and brush. He disappeared into the thick green before Arthur got there.

The fast approaching *wokka wokka* of a helicopter swept their way and sent vibrations drumming up from the ground. This was no MedFlight copter on its way to an accident. He glanced up while running and his toe hit a root or tuft of grass. He tumbled, bags and all. From his sprawl on the ground he looked up. It wasn't coming toward them, yet. It looked like a dark battleship gray private version of a Chinook 47, the kind they call the Mighty Wokka because of its sound. Two big top props, front and back, lowered it to the ground, perhaps for a pickup. As it disappeared down into the tree line far from him he scrambled to his feet and raced to catch up with Frankie.

Frankie waited for him behind a thick stand of hickory trees and leaned out to look back toward Arthur's place.

"What's that about?" Arthur huffed. He still gripped his two small bags and bent to grab his knees and take in deep gulps of air.

"It's why I was in the airport. It's a 'no fly' zone. Fat lot of good that did. Thought they'd have trouble getting ordnance through too. But you saw how that went."

"Are they dropping off more people at my place, or picking them up?"

Before Frankie could comment a huge hollow *Whump* sounded. Arthur spun in time to see a column of flame and smoke shoot skyward. "My house," he said.

"It *was* your house," Frankie said.

A thing that is suddenly gone from your life, like a house over which you have labored much, takes on a mystic, nostalgic aura when you try to picture it. It comes back to you in scattered bits and pieces, like the highlights and features of an island visited years ago but fondly recalled. Arthur thought of the leather chair where he did most of his nightly reading, the cool stone surface of the breakfast nook where he met each day squarely with coffee cup in hand, the porch where he sat on the rocker through some sleepless summer nights listening to the wind play the tree-top leaves like a harp. Like living on an island, being deep in a woods had its own waves to lull an often rattled person like himself back to calm. Well, all that was decidedly gone now.

He turned to Frankie, and felt his own lips form a tight line. Frankie didn't say anything, just turned and waved Arthur onward. Then Frankie took off at a pace that kept Arthur from speaking for the next twenty minutes to half hour.

They wove up and down hills and stayed in the thick of trees. The underbrush is sparse at this time of year. Drifts of dead leaves littered the forest floor. Every once in a while Frankie stopped to listen, and Arthur felt too thankful for the chance to breathe to speak. Frankie was sure in better shape than Arthur these days.

Only once Arthur had enough air to gasp, "Who *are* those guys?"

Frankie waved him quiet and took off on the run again. In the distance Arthur heard a siren, and then the *whop, whop, whop* of a smaller helicopter. He expected to hear the fierce rustle of whoever was back there coming through the brush after them at any second. All he could hear was his own breath when they slowed again.

At the crest of a hill the thick woods opened up and thinned to sparser vegetation that gave out to fenced-in fields green with thick grass. At least three horses grazed between them and the white farmhouse and red barn below.

"Do you know where you're headed? Frankie asked. He glanced back to Arthur.

"Yeah. My neighbor is Poppy Perkin, used to be Poppy Woods. Do you remember her?"

Frankie peered down at the house. "Sure do. The cheerleader. You had a thing for her once, didn't you? Who'd she marry? Wasn't it Pecky Perkin, the drum major? What a match made in heaven that must be."

Before Arthur could say a word a voice came from behind them. "No one calls him Pecky anymore. That was sophomoric even in high school. His name was Patrick." It was a rich contralto voice. Arthur recognized it, even though it had changed through the years. As it had done many a time back then, it sent a shiver of warm fuzz up his spine, something he could have never admitted to her in a lifetime.

Frankie's head panned back and they saw her at the same time. Poppy Perkin, only she wasn't in a cheerleader outfit, or anything approximating it. She wore jeans and hiking boots, a man's black and white checked flannel shirt knotted at the waist. Her long golden hair was streaked with lines of natural white highlights, silver among the gold, and tied back in a ponytail. Her eyes were, as they'd always been, of an icy blue like a Malamute, intense and penetrating, and they had the same incredible sparkle they'd had as a teen. Being in the sun and laughing a lot had carved some early wrinkles of fine lines on her face. On her they looked good. Some people get even more

27

attractive as they age, and she was one of them. The only thing missing was her constant smile. She looked serious, and that was underlined by the Winchester Model 12 pump shotgun she held in both hands as if she knew how to use it. She held the barrel pointed down, for now, but her finger stayed inside the trigger guard. Arthur couldn't see the safety button, but had to guess it was off. Neither of them made any quick moves.

"You said 'was' about Patrick," Arthur said. "Is he . . .?"

"Dead? Yeah. Three years ago. Cancer. And he never smoked, unless you count an indiscretion or two in college. Hit him like a hammer and he was gone in three weeks, which is a blessing with that sort of thing."

"Look. I'm sorry I didn't make it to the funeral or anything," Arthur said. He hadn't heard about Pecky's death though he kept a sporadic eye on the obituaries, the way people do when they start to outlive one or two of the people with whom they went to school. He had kept the same sporadic eye on anything in the news to do with Poppy, though he would have thought twice about attending the funeral even had he known about it for fear of seeming to be some pitiful eager-eyed bachelor hovering around a widow, especially her, given their past.

"We're going to have to save the chit-chat for later," Poppy said. Arthur remembered her as a bubbling girl, one who had treated him as a pal, a confidant. As a cheerleader she seemed more often than not on the giddy side back then. She spoke with cautious no-nonsense intelligence now. Where had all the years gone?

"What do you mean?" Frankie said. "We've got to get tucked away somewhere. Soon." He glanced back to where thick dark smoke had been rolling up into the sky the last time they had a clear look at the sky.

"You're not going to drag whoever's chasing you this way," she said.

"But we . . ." It was as far as Arthur got before she interrupted.

"You're going to turn left, and make sure you leave a clear trail behind you. Okay? Get moving." She stared at them, and raised the gun barrel a couple of inches.

Frankie took a step, and it looked like he intended to ignore her and go around her until a dog's head poked around a tree. It growled. A Shetland sheepdog may not seem as vicious as a mastiff or a Rottweiler, but this one's ears were all the way back and it looked like it really would bite, bite and enjoy doing so. What made it all the more menacing were its eyes. They were the exact same icy pale blue as Poppy's.

"Easy, François," she said. *Calme.*

To Frankie, she said, "*Il veut bien le faire.*"

"I believe you," he said. "Why is he looking at my crotch?"

"Because that's where he's been trained to bite."

Frankie shrugged. Arthur started to speak, and she shook her head. So he turned and headed the direction she so kindly had suggested.

"When you get clear of the property at the highway, stay low in the thick stand of sumac by the ditch. I'll swing by and get you, and there won't be a trail leading to my place. Okay?"

Arthur turned his head back to say thanks, but she was gone. She and her dog had slipped back into the thick of the woods without a sound. You sure can't depend on cheerleaders to stay the way they were. None of us do, but he had never thought about her having a spine like that. Well, for that matter he had been more than a bit surprised by the change in Frankie.

"You think she named the damn thing after me?" Frankie muttered.

"I don't think so. I do think that we are all of us defined in our character by the things we most want." He hesitated. "If you ask me, her French sounds a little self-taught. I imagine she's spent some time with a textbook or software program making the language the one she shares with her dog. You could test that, but I don't know the phrase for 'Could I please have my testicles back?'"

Frankie—who Arthur suspected spoke French quite well, in dialects if needed—didn't say anything for the three or four miles they hiked, pausing now and again to listen to see if they were being pursued. Arthur could still see smoke coming from where his house had been when he got a glimpse through the trees of the sky. They heard no more helicopter noise, but did hear a couple more sirens, these louder as they got closer to the highway. One doppled by just as they got to the patch of sumac Poppy had described. The leaves were thick and green at the top of the patch, less so near the bottom, so they hung back where they would be obscured from the road. Frankie hunched down, and Arthur crouched beside him, holding his two small bags.

"Kind of ironic that it's Poppy helping us out," Arthur whispered. "She was the one who ratted me out, you know."

"That's right. You got booted out of high school for two weeks in our senior year. Brought beer to school, or something," Frankie kept his eyes on the vehicles going by on the highway.

"No one ever caught me with anything, even though they searched. But her word-of-mouth testimony was enough to get me two weeks of F-sub-sixes in everything. I had to get straight A's to graduate at all."

"I didn't know that," Frankie said. "That you got A's."

"Guidance Counselor told me, 'We knew you could do it. We have your I.Q. on file. Don't know why you were such a slacker.' That sanctimonious ass."

"You *did* bring beer to school, though, right?"

"But they didn't catch me. That's the point. I was ratted out. Any of us who might do that today would think it was funny. I damn near didn't get to graduate back then."

Frankie looked at Arthur, and his expression was hard to read. Whatever he was in the middle of had to be rubbing him hard too. Arthur had just lost nearly everything he owned, so he probably did not have much of a sweet expression himself.

A car pulled up and a door popped open. "Get in quick," she hissed.

They climbed in as fast as they could—Frankie into the back, Arthur in the front—pulled the doors closed behind them and stayed low on the floors. She let off the brake and with a soft chirp of tire squeak slipped back into traffic.

Arthur held his breath for the first mile, but no sirens sounded or chopper blades pounded. That didn't mean they were clear yet.

Chapter Four

Over the hum of the road, which is louder he found when you're hunkered down on the floorboards, Arthur listened for sirens. He took a deep breath. What a time to savor being alive. Try as he might, he could not help thinking of eggs fried in butter until they were crispy brown, with smoked Canadian bacon, chunks of lightly salted muskmelon, fresh-squeezed orange juice, and Sumatra bean black coffee. Now, what the hell did that have to do with anything? Poppy's calm should have reassured him, but it did not. She had her hands on the steering wheel—classic ten o'clock and two o'clock—and stared ahead at the road, only occasionally glancing up at the rear view mirror or down toward him.

He looked away from her. The floor mat so close beneath him looked relatively clean, except for a gum wrapper, occasional bits of hay, dog hairs that probably belonged to François, and a slight smell of horse manure. Poppy didn't seem the gum chewing sort. Perhaps a grandchild was. Well, of course she had grandkids. She had two daughters, both married. He had even seen a picture of Poppy at a parade with one of her grandchildren. He sneaked another look at her. Her eyes stayed fixed on the road ahead.

'

My gosh. She sure didn't look much different than she had in school. That was forty years ago. It seemed like yesterday. He could remember the first time he had seen her give her mouth her signature twist. She still did that, perhaps with more reason than ever now. Back then they were huddled in the library whispering, had already been shushed twice, and she'd been talking about Steve. She often talked about Steve. He had been her regular listener, as if he had no feelings himself. Something she said made him think for a second she was talking about him. That he had a chance. That's when the smile happened for the first time. "You're such a goof." She gave his shoulder a shove. It was a push that had sent him orbiting into forty years of living alone. Oh, there'd been a few girls in college. But he had never gotten past that thought, that original thought that for just a flicker there he had been the one she wanted. Once aware he wasn't, he had listened and had even taken that poke in the eye on her behalf once. He had stayed around, had only gone off his own way later, when she married. Now, here she is, looking almost as if nothing had ever changed. Well, it had. He had learned to get by in solitude and tell himself he liked it. Maybe he did. That he'd bought the place next to hers had been by chance, hadn't it?

He pictured the cloud of dark smoke as it rose above where his home used to be. Crouched on the floor of a moving vehicle, on the run from about every cop in the state, with all his possessions able to fit in a couple tiny bags. He glanced up in time to see her lips take that familiar twist. Yeah, he still admired her, hell, had thought he was in love with her once. That was before she had told on him in high school and got him kicked out for two weeks. What a joke.

When she next glanced down at him with those icy pale blue eyes of hers they weren't laughing. Arthur remembered her as someone who was always in on an inner joke, laughing or smiling constantly. Now she had developed a far sterner look, although one that had some strong character and deep hidden humor behind it. Like many women who are attractive, Poppy seemed to take the words and actions of men at face value until she knew more about them. The questions would start soon. Maybe she could get more out of Frankie than he had. He doubted that.

She had showed cleverness, firm resolve, and resourcefulness when she insisted they draw their tracks away from her place. He had to tip his hat to her about that. His thinking wasn't at its best—Frankie, those men at the airport, his house, explosions. In all, he had had a pretty lousy day and a good load to absorb. What occupied his mind at this precise second was Poppy herself. You see, we all get a little caught up in affairs and sometimes let childhood impressions hang on, unless we get an opportunity or incentive to pop that bubble. He had always thought of Poppy only as a cheerleader, even when he had been more than half dotty about her, as if there was some sort of one-dimensional mold into which she fit. That wasn't like him to be so obtuse, as caught up as he could be in character.

He tried to shift his thoughts away from the seven

agonies he was going through from having to crouch so low. Frankie had been smarter to dive into the back seat where at least he could stretch out across the floor. Sometimes when you are uncomfortable the time seems to stretch. It did so now, until Frankie said, "We've been going for quite a while. We should be to your place by now."

Poppy didn't say anything, just kept her eyes on the road. Her lips tightened.

"We aren't going to your place, are we?" Arthur said. He had pictured them being swooped up by her along the road to throw off anyone tracking them. Then she would take them back to her place. He had a sudden revised picture of them being dropped off at a police station and cops swarming them. She'd ratted him out once before, hadn't she? *Once a tattle-tale, always a tattle-tale.* Okay, maybe he wasn't being fair. Lay it off to stress and just losing his home and not having a clue about what was going on. He began to work through a script of what he might say to whoever took him in. He hoped it wouldn't be the local police or even the sheriff's department. In a rural community he suspected they might be a little antic and over-zealous, a little quick with the night sticks.

"Where are we going?" Frankie insisted.

"Just stay down." This sure wasn't the version of Poppy they'd grown up with.

"You have to tell us."

"I don't *have* to tell you squat," she said. "Just remember who's driving here, and stay low. The road's thick with Highway Patrol and Sheriff's department cruisers. You can't imagine how an airport incident like that's being splashed all over the news. Add a remote country home blowing up and that stirs up these folks."

That kept them both in place on the floorboards. If she wanted to turn them in, all she had to do was to stop the car and point them out.

"So, you're really not taking us to your place?" Arthur said.

"Of course not. They *have* to check there."

She stayed quiet for another mile or two, then said, "You know I've been put in charge of the class reunion next year. It'll be forty years for all of us, and I never thought either of you would show up for it, even with you living right among us, Arthur."

He cocked his head at her. Was she serious? He began to get a Charlie horse in his right calf and reached down to rub it hard.

"A lot of people don't put all that much effort into tracking down missing classmates, but we did. The blank address spots on the mailing list bugged us. So we did some digging, the serious deep drilling kind. You might as well know, Arthur, that Frankie was the hardest person in the whole class to track down."

"It's Frank," he snapped from the floor of the back seat. "You know that."

"Frankie? Pecky? What's in a name, for that matter?" She paused. "After Frank went Special Forces anything about him began to fade until his blip went off the radar altogether. We supposed he'd gone CIA."

"Who's this 'we' you're talking about?"

"I know. Admit nothing. Deny everything. Begin counter-allegations," she said.

"That's FBI. You said he was CIA," Arthur said.

"Neither of you have any idea of what you're talking about," Frank muttered.

"How do you know this stuff?" Arthur asked.

"Vee half our vays," she said in a mock German accent Arthur could quickly tire of.

"Quit kidding around," Frankie snapped.

"Boys, if there *was* ever a time to lighten up and kid around, this is it."

"I still think you're full of it," Frankie muttered.

She ignored him.

"Arthur here was easier to keep track of, since he stayed close. I'll bet you didn't know, Frank, that he's the author of national bestselling thrillers he writes under the penname Aris Aaron. No one's ever met Mr. Aaron, not even his agent according to Mr. Aaron's publicist, and Arthur certainly hasn't shared his secret identity with any of us."

Arthur felt his cheeks flush. She added, "We do know that the library and school system got massive anonymous donations, and that kept us silent."

"Do you really write that potboiler dreck?" Frankie said.

"Are you really a spook going around shooting up airports and getting my home and property destroyed?" Arthur said. It wasn't the snappy comeback he would have liked, but he still stung from being so confused and out of control for the past few hours.

"Arthur the author. How cute," Frankie said.

"Why do you take *her* word for it?" Arthur said. "No one's seen Thomas Pynchon. And J.D. Salinger was a successful recluse all those years. You never saw any literary paparazzi setting up outside their doors."

"I've seen your place. I know how you live now. You didn't have two sticks to rub together when we were kids. I spotted Waterford crystal and imported black granite in that place of yours."

"Former place," Arthur snapped. "Now blown up, because of *you*."

"To tell you the truth, I never cared much for Aris Aaron's books, if that *is* you. They weren't technically up to snuff."

"Not up to snuff? You read them, didn't you, Poppy?"

"You think I wouldn't read them just because I'm testosterone-intolerant?"

Before he could stop himself he said, "Well, nothing I ever wrote prepared me for this."

"Oh, I read your stupid books. The library's full of them. I thought they were okay." She kept her eyes on the road. "They seemed technically all right to me, and they moved along well enough. But I do think they could have been better if you had lived among people instead of being such a hermit out there."

"Could have been better? They were bestsellers."

"I think we all know what *that* means."

Arthur almost asked what she'd accomplished, but she

did have a couple of kids and the grandkids. Besides, she was in the driver's seat and his list of options if she decided to leave him beside the road was not a long one.

"Oh, come on. You've had mixed reviews before. Don't get all huffy on me."

"Yeah, she's your only real supporter here," Frankie chimed in.

"Boys, boys," she said. "I think we have bigger issues to settle here. Frankie." She reverted on purpose to the name that irritated him, "you might have to convince people like Arthur that you're one of the good guys."

"I don't have to say a thing."

"I think you do," Arthur said. "You got me involved and I'm homeless now because of you."

"I think you owe us that," Poppy said. "You're asking a lot of us."

"They should have identified the bodies in the airport by now," Frankie said. "That'll confirm what I'm up against."

"I don't think so, Frankie. You see, the M.E. ended up with only one body of an air marshal who got swept up in the shooting. There were no bodies of the other men in the scuffle, the mystery ones. Those were hijacked before the crime lab folks even got there. I believe you call that 'clean-up' in your trade. If it wasn't for that wrinkle I probably would have turned you both in by now. It hints, just hints mind you, that you might not be the bad guy here. As it is, I'll give you a chance to explain once we get stopped, and it had better be riveting and good or I'll drop dime on both of you in a heartbeat before I let you mess up anyone else around here."

Chapter Five

The vehicle slowed, then stopped. "Stay low," Poppy hissed.

She slid out her door and held the flat of her hand down toward where Arthur crouched on the floor of the passenger's side, the kind of gesture she might use on François. He caught a brief glimpse of a chain link fence at least as high as the one surrounding his own pre-explosion place, only this one had coiled razor wire strung across the top. Along the length of the fence he saw black squares with red lettering, which he guessed were "Posted: No Trespassing" signs. Nice to know he wasn't the only one who valued privacy. A metallic click, then another, and a gate rolled open in a slow clatter.

Poppy hopped back into the driver's seat, repeated her last warning, and started through. The metal gate clanged as it slammed shut behind them, sounding like Fort Knox, or prison.

For the next few moments she followed a long winding drive. Arthur saw the tops of a thick stand of a forest full of old beech, oak, and hickory. He clutched his two small bags.

Arthur tried to recall what section Poppy had been in; not the same one as Frankie and he had shared, he knew that much. Back in the seventh grade their small town school system had done something heinous by today's standards. They'd divided their class into ten sections, 7-1 through 7-10. The upper sections were comprised of the students getting the best grades and, of course, the socially well-off, whether their grades were there or not. Most of the kids in the lower sections had come from "across the tracks," the west end of town divided by railroad tracks that were as real to them in those days as the Berlin Wall. Rod Jeffers, a young black man in what was a pretty segregated white community in those days, had come from that side of town. Though he was in 7-9 or so, his stock rose in high school when he grew to six-foot-five and could bench nearly five hundred pounds. He'd been a great lineman for their school and went on to play for Nebraska and then the Steelers for a year and a half before he blew a knee two weeks before the Super Bowl.

"Do you ever hear from Candy Evans?" Arthur asked.

"Shut up," Poppy snapped at him. She gave him only a quick glare, and if those eyes were drills he would have been Swiss cheese.

Candy Evans had been a cheerleader on the squad with Poppy. A white girl, like the other cheerleaders, she had dated Rod Jeffers for a short while until her father found out and blackened both her eyes and broke one of her wrists in the discussion that followed, before sending her off to a private school. Mr. Evans, Charles, had never confronted Rod, who was a football star, after all.

Arthur wondered what *had* happened to Candy, though it wasn't likely he was going to get an answer soon from

43

Poppy. Perhaps, like so many in their class, she had scattered to the winds. Staying in a small town in Ohio held little promise for most people. Then there were the ones who had heeded the call to war. Given the income levels of the area, and, of course, the draft, the military had attracted quite a few. Viet Nam was in its heyday back then. A number of the other boys, including Frankie, had gone that route, and though most of them had returned, some had not. Others had come back changed. Ben Jarrod, who Arthur had seen once or twice since, still had a tendency to dive under a coffee table if a car backfired or someone slammed a door. Crandall Sampson had come back a skinny marine with an adrenaline Jones. Nothing quite tickled his fancy the way the jungle fighting had. He tried sky diving, white water rafting, and any number of other tom fool things. He finally raced his car alongside a train and shot across its path almost in time. The rest had been in his obit. Most folks, though, thought it wasn't an accident.

Like a lot of people his age, Arthur watched the obituaries with special interest, seeing who had not made it to even date. Paul "Porky" Pearson had lived up to expectations and had died of heart failure a few years ago. Sprightly Sue Ellen McCarthy, who they thought would last forever like some sort of youthful Peter Pan, had surprised them all by getting cervical cancer. There had been a few car accidents along with the tolls of the wars. Mary Franklin, who they all suspected might like girls, died as a Colonel in Iraq, counted a hero by all in local circles. There was even a plaque honoring her next to the cannon on the courthouse lawn.

The car jerked to a halt in a crunch of gravel.

"Is it safe to look out now?" Frankie said.

Poppy glanced to the back seat and suppressed a grin. She was enjoying this. If Arthur hadn't stiffened into a near-permanent crouch he would have popped her one in the ankle. "I guess," she said.

Arthur managed to get the door open and climbed out slowly, straightened and worked the kinks out. He didn't know what he expected, maybe a row of gun barrels pointed at them. They were in the woods, in front of a house that made his own former place look like rustic splendor. There were a few maples, tulip and sassafras trees just getting their spring leaves. Otherwise the setting was similar to where he had lived. The house, though, was a low wooden affair that looked unpainted until you looked closer and realized it was meant to look that way. The vegetation crowded right up to the front of the partial building that pressed against a rock cliff. Even odder, a doe and two fawns stood looking at them in a slightly offended way, as if the underwear of the visitors showed. On the low stoop of the porch an almost perfectly round raccoon sat resting on its back haunches and stared at them in a way that suggested it had copped an even bigger attitude.

"You'd better let me handle this, boys," Poppy said.

She ignored the raccoon and waved to the deer, then slipped around to the side of the house. Arthur did not know if she rang a bell there, or knocked, or what. A front window slid up a few inches and the barrel of a shotgun stuck out.

45

"Who are those with you?" The voice sounded rusty, as if little used.

Poppy came back around to the front, brushing off her jeans, as if she'd been through spider webs. "You know," she said.

"I was afraid of that."

"We need a place for them. Better tend to Scrappy, Huff. He looks ready to bite someone."

"Won't be the first time."

Arthur glanced toward Frankie and caught him giving back the same quick look. That had to be "Dirty Fingernails" Huff Ocher in there. Arthur hadn't heard from him or seen him in years. Few people had.

High above them the wind rustled the beginnings of a leaf canopy in the tree tops, and now that Arthur listened close he could hear the quiet hum of a generator at work.

If there was ever a classmate Arthur could single out as being far more eccentric than himself it would be Huff. He had been the number one science Geek in school, one of those who builds oscilloscopes in his garage and shoots off rockets in the park. In study hall he had made a crystal radio from bits and pieces he had pulled from his pockets. He had generated energy from an old style hand-crank telephone magneto for the fun of shocking others, and once he had nearly killed himself by tapping into a 220 watt line that went past his parents' house. The jolt had knocked him back until he had stretched out on his bed for an hour— with sleeve ends smoldering and hair like Einstein—before he could rise. After high school, Arthur heard Huff had set some sort of record in the Air Force when they handed him a disassembled radio with the task of getting it to work. He had torn up the instructions and put the thing together in about half the time it had ever been done. That was his *milieu*. If they would have asked him to build a satellite Arthur did not doubt that Huff could have done it.

Though it had been a while since Arthur had seen him some things don't change. A hand came out and grabbed the raccoon by the scruff of the neck. The critter had a surprised and outraged look as it was whisked inside. Arthur could hear it kicking up a fuss and making an outlandish amount of noise. When the door opened all the way a few minutes later, Huff stood there. His salt and pepper hair stuck out in many directions, and his eyes had the haunted look of someone who slept little and still hadn't solved all of life's riddles. More than that, he showed the fear, or caution, of someone reluctant to be around humans. Arthur had seen that look himself, in the mirror.

Huff's face had acquired the pasty gray of someone who shunned daylight, and he wore worn sneakers, jeans, and a pale gray sweatshirt, the sleeve of which Arthur could almost guarantee had been used to wipe his nose if old habits held. The main difference was that he had been no stranger to food. His sweatshirt bulged at the chest and waist. He didn't hold out a hand to shake, which was just as well. His personal hygiene had always been a matter of some discussion. He looked at Poppy as if betrayed.

"Why here?" he said.

"It's safest. There's no place else just now." She petted the doe that had come over to her and shoved its head under her hand. The two fawns followed along, but stayed on the other side of their mother. It was unusual for Arthur to see a doe with more than one fawn on his own place, but that wasn't what held his interest at the moment. Huff's gaze had skipped lightly over Arthur, but when it landed on Frankie his expression shifted into one that held what Arthur could only call malice. This from one of the easiest going persons Arthur had ever known.

Arthur glanced toward Frankie, who stared back at Huff with much the same expression, of tasting something sour. "Do you mean to say *he's* on your little team?" Frankie said.

Before Poppy could respond, Huff said, "Are you saying a techno-nerd has no place on a reunion committee? Where were you when Poppy was looking for help? Off too busy, in worlds far more important than this one?"

"I'm just saying why *you*, in particular."

"Well, for one, I know encryption. Some class members were hard to locate."

"Yeah, like you could crack some of the most secure systems in the world."

"I know about you in Venezuela, Frankie. Quite a little mess you left behind there."

Frankie's mouth reverted to the pinched tight line it could get. He was done talking.

Huff turned to Arthur and Poppy. "Think about it. Like ourselves, Frankie is a little too long in the tooth to be an active part of any spy force. It's the same principle that applies to why you don't see many middle-aged Olympic competitors. He'd probably be riding a desk if he was still with any of the agencies that would have him. I did hear that some of the agencies were calling back older agents to help at places like good old Guantanamo Bay since the younger agents lacked the kind of interrogation experience—translate that "torture"—needed there. Frankie, though, wasn't in Cuba. He's more likely on his own hook and has been for some time, doing what freelance work he can get in his line. You note I didn't say mercenary. But it amounts to the same thing."

Frankie looked away, declining even eye contact now. Arthur mulled over how Huff seemed uncharacteristically brave, given how fit and ready for rough work Frankie looked.

"Well," Poppy said, "maybe you can help us figure out what Frankie is up to."

"I already know," Huff said.

"How can you?" she said. When she wanted to, Poppy could sure shift her mouth into a twist that said she was on the inside of some deeply ironic joke. That wasn't her look this time. She looked as startled as Arthur felt.

Frankie said nothing. His stubborn glare intensified, but there was little new in that. You can get that kind of look at an IRS office, or at some DMVs, and there was little doubt that Frankie worked for the government, or had in the past.

Whatever was on Huff's face made the deer skittish, and they backed up a couple of steps, as if getting ready to dart. Arthur looked around. The woods, as far as he could see in any direction, looked green and peaceful. Yet the hush cast a pensive mood that may have been real or imagined. Such was his state of mind at the second that if a SWAT team or group of paratroopers had stormed in at them from any direction Arthur wouldn't have been in the least surprised. He would need new underwear, but he wouldn't be surprised.

"Stay here," Huff said, and slipped back inside.

That left Poppy, Frank and Arthur staring at each other in awkward silence. At least the deer moved back closer where Poppy could resume rubbing the doe's head.

Only a couple or three longish minutes went by until Huff burst back out of his front door with a gadget in his hand—a small hand-held white box going to a cone at one end. He shuffled over toward Frank, who took half a step back before stopping himself.

Huff glanced Arthur's way and answered the question in his eyes. "It's an alpha radiation detector."

"But, what do you . . .?" Before Arthur could finish, Poppy waved him quiet and stared toward Frankie and Huff.

Huff waved the cone end near Arthur and got a low static, like a bad radio connection. Then he swept the cone end up and down Frankie and the noise that came from the gadget grew loud and crackled like a forest fire.

Frankie's mouth tightened into a thin line, while Huff looked back toward Poppy and Arthur. "I don't like to point fingers," Huff said, "but one of us is lit up like a neon fart."

Chapter Six

Steve Hamilton sat behind his desk half turned toward the window, from which, if he walked to it, he could see shining glimmers of the Potomac River. He'd just had his 65-foot Carianda Gold Coast Flybridge Yacht fueled and made ready. If he made the seventeen-and-a-half minute drive over to his slip, traffic providing, with just the ready money he had on hand or could quickly muster, he wondered how far he could go, how long he could be away? He sat right on the razor's cusp of finding out. But the Caribbean or any of the other places he could imagine still wouldn't calm the restless gnawing he felt inside. Oh, he'd see this damned thing through yet. He'd stay and fight and scrap, go down swinging if he had to. He wished he could deal with things like Rolly. Take Boris, his personal trainer. "I don't want to do three more damned sit ups, Boris," he'd said. "I don't at this precise second ever want to do another goddamned single sit up of any kind, shape, or form. Hear me? You're sacked, Boris. Do you savvy *that*?" When what he really wanted to do was grab a ten pound dumbbell in each hand and hammer Boris' smarmy head into a jelly of broken skull and smiling ultra white teeth on the very sweaty mat where Steve lay stretched out, too exhausted to get up. That's how Rolly would do it.

Bam, bam, bam. Of course, Steve had hired Boris in the first place, and asked him to be tough. But damn.

He wrenched away from the block of blue sky he could see and went back to the work on the desk in front of him, but he looked up when the door opened. "I thought you had everything contained, Rolly?" Rolly wore some Jungle Jim sort of bungalow or safari shirt with khaki slacks. Steve had at least loosened the Windsor knot of his tie and opened the top button. His jacket hung on a walnut valet to his left.

"Did. It came uncontained. But we'll get it." Rolly didn't look right at Steve. He walked across the burgundy carpet of the office to the 15th Century black walnut sidebar and reached for the bottle of Wild Turkey beside a row of turned-down shot glasses. He poured himself a jolt and looked toward the desk.

"You know how early it is?" Steve said.

Rolly nodded toward the pile of spreadsheets on the desk. "You still cussing at Enron for making you keep your nose clean." He glanced out the window. Still not a lot to see of Bethesda from the fourteenth floor. A gull swept by in the otherwise clear pale blue sky.

"Don't even start to screw with me, Rolly. I'm in no piss-ass mood. So don't even start, especially since security is your bailiwick, and your line item on the cost side of the sheet." The thing about great fortune is that it only happens with great risk. *Nothing* can go wrong. It's like driving a multi-billion dollar tanker through a storm only to find you have a crack in the hull. Since nine-eleven security costs had increased by a factor of ten, giving electricity a run on being his most expensive plant cost. Rolly might understand a glimmer of how that felt from his days in the ring as a golden glove boxer, only for Steve it was like having dozens of opponents, hundreds of them, all wanting him to fail, doing all they could to make that happen.

"I had everything going along fine except for one or two people I thought we could most trust."

"There's a lesson here, Rolly. Don't ever hire someone from your own class."

"I was in your class too."

"That's different. I mean like Paul."

"I took care of Paul."

"We still have another loose cannon, though, one you were *supposed* to have spiked."

"I will," Rolly said.

"Better pour me one, and tell me what went wrong."

"Just luck, dumb luck. You can't find cunning anywhere in this. This should have been clean, and quick."

"Luck shouldn't be any part of this. Hear me?"

"I'm warming up the jet. You coming?"

"I'm supposed to meet with the board." He took the shot held out to him and knocked it back with a tilt of his wrist. Might as well have been soda with the carbonation gone flat.

"Suit yourself."

"I thought we agreed we need to be seen here."

"I have to go. You should too."

"Your men can't handle this?"

Rolly stared back at him.

"I can put the meeting off. That's not it. What's so hot

we need to be over there?"

"It's turning into a bigger snarled mess than I'd hoped. I'd better brief you on the plane. I already loaded you a spare change of clothes. Coming?"

"Well, I guess I had better. Damn it to hell."

Chapter Seven

Huff's gray sweatshirt swelled until he looked, for a moment, like a pouter pigeon about to explode until he took a breath and his chest settled back to his waist. His furrowed eyebrows stayed pinched, though. Arthur had never seen Huff with his back up before. In school he had been the creampuff sort of nerd, more interested in science than a fight. But he sure looked like he might just bite Frankie at the moment. Frankie, in response, had gone all tight-lipped and glared back. Arthur would have to bet on Frankie if it came to blows, unless Huff fell on him.

Poppy glanced around at the woods surrounding them. Aside from a "rare to see in the daytime" possum that wandered out into the clearing, saw them, and turned to waddle back into the thick green of low shrubs, nothing moved. Poppy looked like she wouldn't be surprised to see a SWAT team in full gear spring out at them. "I think we should go inside," she said, "until we can sort all this out."

"Why my place?" Huff said again.

"Because my place is right next to Arthur's. After the explosion there, mine is the first house and property they will check. Besides, I don't have the perfect place to stow two as hot as this. You do."

"Not the safe room?"

"I'm afraid so. Don't worry. I'm sure they'll be glad to chip in for any of your precious supplies they use."

"I'm not sure I care to stay here," Frankie said.

"I don't think you have much of a choice, Bucko," Poppy said. "Better step lively now."

Arthur could have commented on the assertive changes Poppy had made in her life, but the look she gave him shut him up too, and he stepped along with the others as Huff spun on a reluctant Converse All Star heel and sulked toward the shack he called home.

The deer ambled off to feed on tall grass at the edge of the clearing. A woodpecker flittered from one tree top to the next, and the wind tugged at the tops of trees against a sky that was beginning to darken. Arthur doubted he could begin to comment on the why and what of everything going on around him.

He did what many people do when pressed beyond their limits. He began to revert to what he did most often, write stories in his head that later become the novels he had been getting published. Take Frankie there. He possessed something that was hard to figure, but was attractive to a writer in an oxymoronic way. Arthur had been wanting to work with a character who was schizophrenic to a bipolar level—part of him driven by an over-achieving will to succeed, to win at all costs, the other half dominated by a deep abiding sense of raw humility that struggled to hold him back all the while. Aside from being the old spy who came in from the cold, Arthur wondered how much of the character edge he saw in Frankie was really there. No matter, he could craft it, shape it some and use it, if he ever got out of this.

Huff reluctantly opened the front door. Poppy followed him in, with Frankie close behind. Arthur brought up the rear and closed the door, then looked around at the room and nearly rocked back on his heels. The inside of what was a shack on the outside could have been a small scale entry to the pages of *Architectural Digest*, complete with white walls, sparse but pristine furniture, marble surfaces, and a low fireplace where flames crackled over what smelled like real wood burning.

"What's the matter?" Huff said to Arthur. "Not what you expected. Maybe I took a hint or two when you portrayed a character in your books that could have easily been modeled after me, complete with a chronic dose of halitosis you so politely referred to as 'stronger than napalm.' Well, smell my breath now."

Arthur pulled his eyes away from a room that was a considerable cut above what his own place had been and saw Huff staring at him.

"He's serious," Poppy said. "Smell his breath."

"Are you kidding?"

"Better do it," Frankie smirked, "or we'll be at this all day."

Arthur panned their faces once more, and ended on Huff, who leaned forward, expectant. Arthur sighed and stepped close, bent toward Huff's mouth.

"Well?" Huff said.

"Minty fresh," Arthur admitted.

"Now, can we get on with whatever," Frankie said.

Poppy struggled to hold back a grin. Huff led the way into the next room, clearly his *sanctum sanctorum*. Screens covered one wall. Live feeds from a dozen television stations, all with the sound off, surrounded a low row of computer screens along a long desk that ran along one wall. The other wall was lined with file cabinets topped by book shelves crammed with books ranging from the Rosicrucian history to Roswell, UFOs to secret societies, from alien abductions to JFK. Government reports appeared to be sprinkled in among the non-fiction books and boxes of carefully archived magazines. As a pretty good researcher himself, Arthur would have warned him away from the secondary sources.

"Still a conspiracy theory nut?" Frankie asked. The corner of his mouth tugged up even farther. "Still learning all you can about the grassy knoll?"

"Don't get him started on the grassy knoll," Poppy cautioned.

Huff glared at Frankie. His hands balled into rough fists. Yet he knew better than to start anything with Frank. This current Frankie had an edge to him Huff wasn't all the way up to challenging.

"Still claiming the moon landing was a hoax?" Frankie goaded.

"I have only one question for you," Huff said with strained dignity. "The so-called man-on-the-moon incident happened in July of 1969, complete with a flag that flapped in an environment with no wind. All six alleged Apollo missions happened between then and 1972, all during the presidency of Richard Milhous Nixon, a man few remember for his honesty. You think those missions couldn't have been staged in some movie studio lot for a whole lot less money than flying them, all for a cold war coup? So you tell me. Why hasn't there been another single mission to the moon by us or anyone else in all this time since? NASA says we don't even have the capabilities now. How was it we did then?"

Poppy tapped one foot and waited for Huff to calm down. Arthur looked around at the room in which Huff spent the most time.

A bunk bed stood against the back wall of the room with both its top and bottom beds neatly made. It seemed an odd choice until Arthur thought about it. That had to be the same bed Huff had brought from his parents' home, the bed he'd had all his life, the one he'd grown up with. There was not much Arthur felt like saying about that.

Next to the bed stood a thick steel door in a steel frame. Frankie spotted it at about the same time Arthur did.

"Oh, my Lord. You *do* have a panic room." Frankie glanced around at the walls and the ceilings. No windows. "Let me guess. We're in solid rock here, and that room is even farther into the cliff we saw outside. Probably lead lined, for all that. It's a bomb shelter too. Isn't it?"

If he expected an answer out of Huff he would be a long time getting it. Smoke wasn't coming out of Huff's ears, but it might as well have been from the look he gave Frankie.

"That's right," Poppy said. "It's the one place almost no one searching could find you two, especially given all the love we know Huff has for Frankie and whatever he's up to."

"You've all been pretty damn vague about that," Arthur said, "yet you act like you know and I wish you would tell me. I have a right to know given the extent I'm involved."

Huff shook his head and reluctantly went over to the steel door, bent close so they could see him punch in a combination, but could not make out the numbers. When he swung the door open he glanced to Poppy. "You tell them the rules."

"You have to stay tight here, inside, at least until some of this heat blows over. The phone inside will be cut off and there's the one television, some DVDs and a few books, ones Huff picked out."

Arthur glanced inside. There was a single cot along one wall. "No way," he said.

"Me either," Frankie agreed.

Poppy nodded to Huff, and he took a remote from his pocket and pointed toward the wall of television screens. He started clicking, and with each click the pictures grew more and more dismal. There were road blocks, copter patrols, search dogs; the National Guard had been called out, and the airport closed. That was the statewide scene. The local news was as bad, or worse. Every off-duty cop and deputy had been called in and scores of volunteers helped to comb the woods Arthur knew all too well. One camera picked up a charred spot that was all that remained of where his house had once stood. Abruptly, Huff clicked his remote and all the screens clinked off. When he looked at Frankie this time there was the beginning of a smile, but far from a pretty one.

"I was watching after Nine-Eleven, Columbine and the Virginia Tech situations," Huff said, "and came to the conclusion there's nothing so tragic that the media can't make it comic or boring with enough overkill."

Frankie ignored him and stayed fixed on Poppy.

"So, guys, do you lay low for a little while, or what?" Poppy said.

Arthur looked back inside the small cell where he would be sequestered with Frankie. There was a steel toilet. On the shelves above it were cans of food. A lot of them were tuna. He didn't care much for canned tuna.

Huff caught his glance. "Be careful and go easy on the tuna," he said. "By the year two-thousand-fifty the commercial fisheries of the sea as we know them will be depleted and there'll be no more fish for eating, of any kind we know today."

"I'm not too worried about year two-thousand-fifty," Frankie said, "although whether tomorrow comes or not is up for grabs."

Arthur wandered across the room to the bunk bed and lowered his two bags to the floor and eased himself down to sit on the side of Huff's lower bunk. Huff looked like he wanted to say something, but didn't.

"Look," Arthur said, "I'll go in there, if I have to, and with Frankie if there's no other way. But you *have to, have to, have to* tell me what's going on. You may not know it all, and I doubt if you do. Just give me some scrap so I'm not the only one in the dark here. I've lost a lot, and deserve to know something."

Huff hesitated, looked to Poppy before he spoke. "It's your pal Frankie here," he said. "He was doing the kind of work he does best for Steve Hamilton, for Unitalon."

"Oh," Arthur said. That had been a mouthful. Steve was from their high school class. In fact, he was the richest and most successful one in the whole class, just as the school yearbook editors had said he would be. Only Steve hadn't accomplished it by emulating the path taken by the late Sister Teresa. He had smashed and gutted companies in a way that made Bill Gates and the late Leona Helmsley look like church choir members. When the smoke had cleared at last, according to *Forbes*, he was one of the richest people in America, and the biggest gem of his collection of companies was Unitalon, the company granted exclusive rights in America for all uranium enrichment along with the obligation of waste disposal, and one of his biggest plants was right here in this Ohio county.

"Will any of his radiation rub off on me if we're jammed in that little space for a spell?" Arthur said. "I mean, wasn't something like this used to kill that Russian spy in London?"

Huff grinned at him, as if he had just legitimized all his years of paranoia. He still held the white-coned alpha radiation detector he'd used on Frankie. He swept it up to Arthur and pressed it firmly against his arm. It made only a tiny crackle.

"What killed that Russian spy was polonium-210. It can be found in harmless trace amounts everywhere. It occurs naturally in the earth's crust and is part of the rock that surrounds us. The thing about toxins is the amount. Most toxicology examinations of patients don't begin with radiation poisoning. That gives the patient more time to get worse. If Frankie were to be dosed up far more than he has been he might die of ineptitude in some ER, but he wouldn't hurt you or the doctors who worked on him. You'll be fine in the panic room with him."

"Cell, you mean. It looks like a prison room," Frankie said.

"I shouldn't think that would bother you after Calcutta, Frank," Huff said.

"Now listen," Frankie snapped. "I've about had it with your guesses. Are you trying to make me believe you're able to tap into U.S. Government computers, some of the most secure machines in the world?"

"With ease," Huff said. "It's when we weren't able to get your current status that we knew you'd probably gone over to the private sector. Given your background, and the nature of your past assignments, that meant probably on to work for Unitalon. A little hacking in the right places confirmed that."

"I dispute your information about my files. No one could get access to them."

"Oh, come on, Frankie. If the White Hat Team could do it, I certainly could."

"Just who in the hell is this 'White Hat Team,'" Poppy snapped. She could sure show more of an edge than Arthur would have given her credit for.

"There were a bunch out of Romania—kids, young men

in their twenties," Arthur said, "who made a game out of getting into the files of NASA, the energy department, even the U.S. Navy. Their meddling amounted to disruptions, but little more."

"Well, if it doesn't have anything to do with what we're focused on, let's leave it out of the conversation. Agreed?" There was plenty of fire in those pale penetrating eyes now. Then it hit Arthur. It wasn't just Unitalon on which Poppy was focused.

"You and Steve Hamilton were an item once. That's it," he said. "Back before Pecky, Steve was your childhood sweetheart, your soul mate. I should remember that well enough."

"I'm a long way past believing in soul mates," she said, but the last two words came from behind clenched teeth.

"You were a darn perfect couple, though. Barbie and Ken everyone used to call you. Didn't they?"

Her jaw set and her eyes widened, but she didn't respond. Arthur did hear Poppy mutter low under her breath, "Please, please let this be what I think it is."

Until that very moment Arthur had had no idea why she was helping them. Now he saw the glimmers of fury that can only come from an extremely jealous and angry woman who had been scorned.

She caught Arthur's glance and the emotion left her face. "You must feel like you've been shot at and missed and shit at and hit. Huff, do you have any beer in your ice box?"

He nodded.

"I'll get our boys here a round." She hurried out of the room.

Arthur would have preferred a glass of red wine, and his easy, chair, and perhaps a fire in the fireplace. He sighed.

Frankie looked at him. "What do you think?" he said.

Arthur shook his head. "That they sure don't make cheerleaders like they used to."

*   *   *

Poppy stepped out of Huff's house and worked her way out onto the lawn to stand alone in the dark. The vague shapes of a few night critters rustled among the leaves of the thick underbrush. Sensing she was not Huff they ambled away before Poppy got her night eyes and could tell what they were.

A firm breeze tugged her hair across her face and she gave it an irritated sweep away from her eyes with one hand. The stars were sure bright out here. She could make out constellations, but didn't know their names. Huff probably did.

The wind brushed cool against her skin. Her face felt flushed to the roots of her hair and the breeze felt good, though it did little to calm the fire within.

She tried to focus on the things that mattered, what she had left behind to participate in this. She had left food out for the horses and François, but she should be checking the mare's stitches. She needed to check the calendar too and see when they were due to be wormed. The back forty acres of pasture lining the creek that led into the thicker woods had thick grass that had grown knee high. Time to fire up the John Deere and bush hog it. The barn could use painting too. *Oh, who was she kidding? She could no more change the subject on herself than she could change who she was and just how she felt.*

They all knew. The minute that damned Mary Ann Reznick showed up at school with the money green glow of her daddy's mining concerns in a dozen states in an aura around her, Steve's head had snapped like a hound catching a scent.

Of all places in America to settle why they had to settle out here was beyond her. Maybe it was so rich old pop could play at being the big frog in a small pond, and build a literal fucking castle, the most exotic estate any of the locals had ever seen. You couldn't miss the idiot thing. Red-capped white turrets of the castle towered up through the trees that surrounded the old tourist cave the Reznicks had closed to the public. A stupid, honest to God castle that came as a result of a promise Mary Ann's father had made to her mother. It even had a moat, along with a drawbridge that worked. Mary Ann was its resident princess too and apparently used to getting what she wanted, and she had wanted Steve. Sure, Steve had kicked a bit at first, but he could sure see and smell that folding currency that made such a warm green glow behind Mary Ann. It was always money with Steve. Mary Ann had known the exactly right bait, and soon she and Steve were the school's hot item, and that let Poppy and her childhood sweetheart dream out.

Steve dumping her for Mary Ann Reznick was the low point of her high school life. The utter bottom. She had cried and cried and then cried some more until she felt turned inside out, until even Pecky began to look good. Sure, she had married Pecky, and though he meant well enough he had always seemed a shadow of what she had wanted, what she had thought she had coming to her. What was hers.

A lot of people don't believe in soul mates, but she had been one who did. *Then.* A lot of times when she closed her eyes it had been Steve making love to her, not poor old Pecky.

She thought all of it had stilled, that she had purged all but a few embers from that fire when she ran into Steve again. She was in her late thirties, and restless. Steve had been restless too. She told herself, "No, no, no" all the way up until she opened her eyes in the bedroom of a Plaza Hotel Suite and Steve was there. She realized she had been saying, "Yes, yes, yes."

Everything that had happened before seemed erased, and they kidded about it. The flames leaped higher than ever for seven months. They schemed and met where they could, did things they would never have dared done as kids, explored levels she hadn't known existed. Then Steve needed money again, and along came that damned Astrid Lazo with oil millions in her family. Like that, a cold door slammed closed on Poppy again.

If she thought she had cried before that had only been practice. This time she had bawled and moped until the slightest thing would send her off. Poor Pecky did what he could, blamed himself, and went from being frustrated to angry to becoming a morose drinker. He never knew. That poor sweet man had died thinking he had been the one to screw up. She had wanted to tell him, had even tried, started to confess once or twice. Now she had to live with the guilt that she had been unkind to a good man, a kind man. She could never, never tell him how she felt, what she appreciated about him. God, how that gnawed at her.

She had been a long time coming clear after the second time with Steve. But she had learned something. If they were soul mates she could expect to meet him in hell. She had come to understand a passion far bigger and stronger and bolder than love. She now knew how to hate.

Chapter Eight

Arthur woke up to the sound of voices.

"There's enough here to really do some things." Poppy's voice.

"That's some serious scratch." A much, much deeper voice, neither Huff nor Frankie.

Arthur sat up so abruptly he hit his head on the upper bunk. The lights from the multiple televisions flickered in the otherwise unlit room, but he could make out where they were huddled and going through the bags he had brought with him, all that remained of his world.

"What the hell are you doing?" Arthur said.

He remembered arguing about spending the night with Frankie in the tiny panic room with one cot. He couldn't picture that steel-on-steel door clanging shut behind them, making them as much trapped as protected. It had loomed as claustrophobic a notion as he could imagine. Somewhere along there, sitting in the warm room, dead tired after a day from hell, he had grown groggier and groggier, must have konked out on Huff's bed. They'd let him, or had Poppy put something in his beer? Now they were going through his things.

Arthur blinked again, this time because he realized that Frankie had just taken his arm from around Poppy's side and had taken a step back. Poppy wore no lipstick, but Frankie reached up to rub a forefinger across his lower lip. The cold wet fish slap of reality biffed Arthur up the side of his head once more in the space of very little time.

Arthur stood up, hands balled up in fists at his sides. "Someone's got a hell of a lot of explaining to do, and right now."

Huff grinned, as did the big fellow who hung over his shoulder looking down into Arthur's bags.

"Rod? Rod Jeffers, is that you?"

"Sure enough is." He stood up straight. He'd been quite a solid slab in high school, but not this size. He looked pro football lineman large now, and hadn't been ignoring the gym either.

"I don't care how big you are or how many of you there are. I'm going to be kicking some major butt here in one minute unless I get some straight answers." Arthur realized he shouted, and it was not that big of a room, so his voice really boomed. "I'm not going to be anyone's patsy. Understand?" Spray shot from his lips with the last shouted word, but he didn't care.

"Good," Poppy said, with a pursed mouth and nod to herself. "That's the most spirit you've shown so far. We may need more of that. Pecky, it turned out, could be something of a wimp. We wouldn't want more of that from you, especially now."

"If he was such a wimp," Arthur shouted, drawn

70

completely off the subject at hand, "why'd you marry him?"

"I think you know the answer to that."

"Because Steve Hamilton wouldn't have you." There was a second or two of utter quiet in the room after Arthur yelled that.

Poppy almost shot out of her chair. Her hands were bent like two claws. She caught herself, slowly relaxed, and eased back down. "No. It wasn't that at all."

Frankie gave Arthur his own crooked grin. "We're going to have to trust each other here, so you might as well know what's going on," he said.

"Do you *think?*" Arthur was still furious enough to broadcast a tiny spray of spittle with each word. On any other occasion it might have been cute, like Daffy Duck or Donald having one of their trademark arm-waving sputtering temper snits. He noticed the turned-head glare Huff gave Frankie, one that was far from filled with love. He didn't know why, but that made him feel an ounce or two better.

"What a day you've had," Poppy said. "Killed someone in a public place, had your home blown up, and had your secret identity revealed." She waved a hand up to the flickering television screens, where in at least two cases Arthur now saw a photograph of himself being shown, but not one of Frankie. "That does blow large chunks," she said.

Arthur opened his mouth, then closed it without saying anything.

Frankie winked at Arthur. "I've always thought you

needed more realism in your books, something you can't get off living like a hermit. Getting along without a shell will be good for you. Think how you'll write after this."

Arthur knew he must look pissed off enough right at that moment to commit almost any outrage.

Rod stood up all the way until he towered over the others and Arthur. He squared his shoulders and waited, in case this came to blows. He looked like he didn't want to hurt Arthur, but couldn't promise anything if Arthur did something crazy.

Arthur was breathing hard, panting really. Years ago, in college, he had been forced, by the poverty of student life, to buy a brand of wine at the Big Bear grocery called something like Vino del Primo. It ran about four dollars a gallon and came in a pretty nice jug at that. It was so awfully bad that the first three glasses or so would always make him shudder, and he could swear it had gone a ways toward taking the enamel off his teeth. But the shudders he had felt then were nothing to what he felt now as the awareness of the soup he was in swept over him.

"Why isn't Frankie's picture up there too?" Arthur finally managed, nodding toward the screens. That they were going through his things and practically counting his money meant little to him compared to being a fugitive from the law. In a single day he had gone from being a respected citizen, one who kept and desired as low a profile as a person could get, to being public enemy number one in the news.

"You see," Frankie said, still as calm as the center seed

in a cucumber low on a vine away from the sun, "the thing is that I no longer exist. Technically, I've been dead for over a year now."

"It just seems that way," Poppy said, "in bed."

"I can do without the humor, Poppy," Arthur snapped. She still had a slim, muscular figure, and the silver highlight streaks of hair added more sparkle to her long blond hair than gave away her years. She looked even better to him now than she had as a cheerleader. Yet that didn't make him want to imagine any scenes of rampant intimacy between her and Frankie, a concept that, in spite of himself, made his blood warm.

"Those were Steve Hamilton's men at the airport, then?" he asked.

"We're pretty sure they were," Huff said. This coming from a conspiracy theory nut. That was sweet.

"And what are you doing here, Rod? On the reunion committee too?" Arthur said.

"Of course. Frankie isn't, but Poppy, Huff and I are."

"Do you want on?" Poppy asked. "We've had a recent opening."

"I hate to dash the cup of joy from your lips, Poppy, but right at this moment I could care less if there ever *is* any damned reunion. I haven't seen the lot of you guys in years, and I haven't felt I've missed all that much."

"You're going to have to see us now, and be with us," Rod said in that quiet deep voice of his, "because you need us. Look, we know you're as squirrelly as a pile of dog shit, always have been, but you're still one of us. We've been helping insulate you all these years. We knew who was behind those hefty anonymous contributions that gave us a new library and one of the best school systems around. But we said nothing to give you away, and we won't now."

"Give him a few minutes," Poppy said. "He's still getting over having killed someone for the first time."

"A gut reaction," Frankie said. "He did it spur of the moment."

He was right about that, and it had been to protect someone who Arthur didn't particularly like, who he just happened to know. Now Frankie stood there in front of him willing him to diminish the one thing he had done that could either be the most right or the most wrong thing he'd done in his life.

"Oh, don't give me that look. You'll find soon enough, if you don't already know, that you can't make everyone happy, no matter what you do," Frankie said.

"Look, I just want to know whose side I'm on."

"That's the thing, you see," Frankie said. "There aren't really any sides to this."

"What do you mean?"

"You'll find out soon enough that everyone is against you, at least in the mess I'm in, that you're in too now."

Arthur glanced to Poppy, Huff and Rod. They looked expectant, as if he was about to make some sort of a decision.

"I agree with him," Poppy sighed. "We need to tell him more."

"What if he decides to take a flier?" Rod asked.

"He doesn't have a choice. None of us do," Frankie

said. He looked away from Arthur, with that irritated grimace that was really starting to rub Arthur raw.

Huff cleared his throat. Just the voice of reason Arthur was eager to hear from, the guy with forty televisions going and a wall of files on things no one cared about.

"Do you believe our government regulates businesses, or that the businesses really run our government?" Huff said, then shrugged and went on before Arthur had a chance to respond. "It doesn't matter. The fact is that around here I think you know what business showed up and buttered most people's bread, and with every bit of good news there's some bad news."

"You don't have to make a sermon out of it," Rod interrupted. "What's the biggest business in this county?" he asked Arthur.

"The nuclear plant," Poppy answered for him. "Right in the middle of our quiet Ohio woods we have the largest uranium enrichment plant in America. Sure, there was kicking when it came in, but the promise of jobs and revenue rolled over any resistance that the advance PR didn't take care of. It's been a fact of life we've all grown up with and lived with."

"And a fact of death," Huff said.

"He knows about the PCBs, trichloroethylene, toxic fluorine, even plutonium in the unlined ponds and landfills and bone cancer and leukemia that have affected hundreds," Poppy said. "He'd have to be living in a hole not to hear about that."

"He *has* been living in a hole," Huff said.

She gave him a quieting glance, her expression shifting

75

as she panned back to Arthur. "Huff's dad had to have his larynx removed after the cartilage was attacked by a rare form of bone cancer caused by inhaling radioactive substances during his lifetime of work at the Gaseous Diffusion Plant. He had an ElectroLarynx installed, a voice prosthesis that amplified the vibrations of his throat."

"Made him sound like a damned robot," Huff said.

"When he underwent surgery to remove part of his lung for the cancer that reoccurred, he died on the operating table. You need to know," Poppy said, "he was a health nut who exercised and never drank or smoked."

"Do you know what they gave him? *A hundred and fifty thousand.* That's what his life was worth." Huff stopped when he noticed his voice was starting to boom in the small room.

"The government?" Arthur asked.

"It was *then*," Poppy said, "before handing the nuclear program over to the private sector. Do you recall the Energy Employees Occupational Illness Compensation Act?"

"Not specifically."

"It passed in 2000. That's when the cash payments to the workers or their eligible survivors started."

"To give you a feel for how that's working," Huff said, "of nearly sixty thousand applicants, only fifteen percent got any money or medical benefits."

"And *that's* what this is about?" Arthur said.

"No. That damned hand-washing government . . ." Huff looked like he had more to say, but he got waved quiet by

Poppy. If Arthur had had any doubts before about who was in charge here, those were being quickly dispelled.

"Look, if you guys are just eco-nuts out on some kind of environmental crusade, power to you," Arthur said. "But count me out. I've got issues of my own."

"No, you don't. They're the same issues," Poppy said.

"You're saying that the business at the airport, what led to my fix, has to do with the nuclear plant that's been an albatross around the neck of this county for as long as we've lived here?"

"That's right." Poppy didn't look smug, which was to the good. "You know as much about the history of the plant as any of us."

Yeah, Arthur knew it too well. The plant had started up about the time each of them was born. It's a wonder none of them had three eyes. It had been run for about thirty years by the Goodyear Atomic Corporation, was taken over by a subsidiary of Martin Marietta in the eighties, which evolved into Lockheed Martin in the nineties. "All the companies acted as operators of a government-own plant until the whole mess was privatized in ninety-eight to Unitalon," Arthur said. "All this brings us back to Steve Hamilton. If you think something's rotten in Denmark there, why not call in the feds?"

"The feds are not your friends," Huff said. "Believe me when I say that. Who do you think handed over 50 years worth of federal investment in potentially dangerous nuclear technology to Unitalon, as a gift? The FBI and other agencies want the plant to succeed."

"The local law then?"

Poppy let out an unladylike snort. "I think you know what we're up against there. They're not your friends either."

"It's just us," Rod said. "We had two more. Wally Moon is over at the plant now, with some of Huff's surveillance equipment. Then there's Paul Felsenfeld. Do you remember him?"

"Remember him? I just saw him at the grocery two weeks ago. He still plays softball and bowls. What do you mean do I remember him?"

"He didn't make it out. He worked inside," Rod said. He barely got the words out. His voice crackled with suppressed emotion.

"Didn't make it out?" Arthur repeated.

"We think he's dead," Poppy said.

Chapter Nine

"What do you think happened to Paul?" Arthur asked.

"We don't know, for sure," Poppy said, "All we knew was that one minute he was around, then his blip suddenly went off the radar."

"Literally," Huff said. "I had a GPS tracker in one of his sneakers. He was at the plant, then neither he nor his sneaker existed anymore."

"No one's seen him since," Rod said. He nearly choked over the words. His being so large made the show of emotion all the more unexpected. "The local law, in their own feeble way, went through the routine missing-person drill. But pop. He was just gone." He ended on what sounded like a soft hiccup.

"You think Steve Hamilton's responsible? Or someone at his plant?" Arthur said.

"We know so," Huff said. "Don't we, Frank."

Frankie hesitated. He had been nothing but calm so far. "You see," he finally said. "I'm a witness. But I can't turn myself in because I doubt if I can trust anyone. I'm a loose end Unitalon needs to snip if it's to stay remotely squeaky clean in the public's eyes. And, of course . . ."

"I get it," Arthur said.

"Yeah, you're tied to that now too," Huff said to

Arthur. "Even if you turn yourself in something would almost certainly happen to you, something you wouldn't care for."

"There's only one way out," Poppy said, "for Frankie, and you. You have to prove what Steve and Unitalon is up to."

"So you didn't whisk me out here to Huff's just to hide me from the law." Arthur looked toward Poppy. "There's a lot more to this story, isn't there?"

"Frank had long ago switched over from his— government work—to a senior security job with Unitalon," Poppy said, "and just recently he was in the wrong place at the wrong time."

"I've been on the run since Paul disappeared, and they only got wind of me again when I came back to Ohio." Frank glanced to Poppy. "I shook their copter at the 'no-fly-over' zone of the airport, and didn't count on their getting that many weapons past security."

"Steve's men are the ones who whisked the bodies of their own men out after the airport shooting? Right under the noses of the feds?" Arthur pictured once more the man flying backwards after he had shot him.

"Unitalon is twice more desperate and dangerous than any federal agency. They're all seasoned pros, like Frankie here. They can pretty much do what they want, with the feds backing them up and helping sweep up after," Huff said. "Your government wants this plant to make it."

"The point is Frank got back inside the plant, and he got close, close enough to pick up some radiation, but he couldn't get the proof he needed," Poppy said. "We knew about it because he'd come to me to hide out, and I told him that Huff was the only person I knew who could begin to help him get into the Unitalon plant here, and that's been tricky."

"You see, there are lasers, light sensors, trip pads—the place is a maze of security now that they're ramping up to do production again," Huff said. "Meanwhile there are radioactive barrels, soil, and water all around the place that billions of your tax dollars haven't succeeded in clearing up yet. The government is starting to take some responsibility for the past, but they're also green-lighting Unitalon's future, no matter what."

"Stay focused, Huff," Poppy said. "It's the stuff Paul stumbled onto in Bunker F that has Steve and Unitalon's back up enough to do some pretty wild things."

"What's so top secret that Unitalon is willing to kill to keep it quiet?" Arthur looked to Poppy, but Frankie answered.

"Until recently the Pikeburg plant was dead or dying. There were just a few federal workers left on full-time clean-up. Then Unitalon got the bright idea of reviving the American Centrifuge project. It's got everything riding on the project. The company cut jobs, suspended its dividends, and even reduced office space at its Bethesda headquarters. Even so, it'll probably take federal loan guarantees or more outright aid for the company to make it at all. Everything is riding on this gamble, and it takes place right here at your local plant."

"*Our* plant," Rod rumbled. "You're from here too."

"I've heard glimmers," Arthur admitted, "but I don't understand the whole thing. Even my usually good contacts had come up blank on the subject."

"You'd better explain, Huff," Poppy said. "You know the tech side of this best. But do try to keep our feet on the ground."

Huff turned to Arthur with more eagerness than Arthur could have wished for. "Centifuges have been around for years, but Unitalon claims its super-tall, ultra-fast centifuges will allow the United States to become the world leader in uranium enrichment technology. Unitalon wants to replace the 1940s technology at the Pikeburg plant with twelve-thousand forty-three foot high machines that separate uranium isotopes with centrifugal force for power that can be used to make electricity—or bombs."

"Huff," Poppy warned.

"Well, it's the exact same technology that leaked out onto the black market and ended up in the hands of North Korea in 2006, and the same technology used in Iran that got that country a United Nations sanction."

"Tell him about the down side," Rod encouraged.

"The fact is that Pikeburg *had* a centrifuge program until 1985, when it closed it down after the Three Mile Island incident. Even the government's centrifuge people give the new twist for this plant a fifty-fifty chance of making it." Huff glanced to Poppy.

"Yet Unitalon is pushing ahead, and becoming more desperate all the while. Standard & Poor's slashed Unitalon's credit rating all the way into junk territory, which means Hamilton will have an even harder time raising money. He's the kind of guy who needs to succeed at all costs." The prospect of Steve failing made her wrestle to suppress a smile. "The other side of Unitalon's time bomb is the arrangement with the Russians."

"That's another side of the sweet deal Unitalon was gifted," Poppy said. "The U.S. government *gave* the company the exclusive arrangement—a monopoly—to sell uranium from Russian warheads."

"Did you know that Russia supplies half of Unitalon's enriched uranium?" Huff said. "The company then supplies the converted low-enriched uranium to about a hundred and fifty reactors worldwide. That's a lot of Russian input, and there's a timeline end to the arrangement coming, and when that happens the Russians will dump Unitalon as a middleman and flood the market with their uranium."

"As much as I hate to fuel Huff's crazed conspiracy bent," Frank said, "this *is* a deal that stinks. The U.S. signed an eight-billion dollar deal with Russia after the collapse of the Soviet Union to buy its warheads to turn the already weapons-grade enriched uranium in them into fuel-grade uranium. It's known as the Megatons-to-Megawatts deal. On the surface it sounds okay. Gets warheads out of possible circulation and gets us energy. But your tax dollars are at work twice. After the U.S.'s nuclear energy program was privatized, as Unitalon, the DOE subsidizes Unitalon's costs to keep the deal working. You see, Russia would like out of the deal so it could sell to other buyers, like Iran. The U.S. government wants the plan to stay until it expires in a few years, to keep Iran and others out of the nuclear game, which is probably too late. So the feds want Steve's company to prosper and grow."

"And this whole complex string of events leads to my airport incident?" Arthur said.

"Right," Huff said. "Back when Unitalon was a government-owned business it hired Steve. He went from acting as a consultant to becoming Unitalon's CEO. In 1998, while still government-owned, the company had a choice of selling out to a giant company like Lockheed Martin or spinning off a for-profit company with Steve Hamilton as its head. In a behind-closed-doors meeting, which Steve by the way was allowed to attend, he got the go-ahead and the billion dollar company was handed to him on a platter in one of the most stinky government deals ever to go down. With that came the arrangement with the Russians."

"Here's the thing, you see," Poppy leaned closer and those unblinking icy eyes got even more intense, "Paul was working in there. He knew just enough to have suspicions that Unitalon wasn't converting *all* the warhead uranium. He nosed closer and found that during the construction Steve had a few bunkers built, not for safety, or waste, so why would Steve, who loves money, go through the expense. You can't imagine the scrutiny a place that this is under, yet Steve managed to bit-by-bit set aside a cache of highly-enriched uranium, weapons-grade, enough to make a couple of warheads. It's being held back in one of the bunkers, Bunker F, like some sort of hole card for Steve. If these new centrifuges don't work, or if they don't get them built on time, or if they take more electricity than projected and the whole thing isn't profitable, then it looks like Steve has a Plan B. All he has to do is contact a bidder or two in the rest of the world, where America has become a less-than-loved nation. It's enough to make us suspect he might even have been the one to leak technology information to North Korea and Iran too, though we can't prove any of that. But if he has highly-enriched uranium set aside to hedge his bet, which we think he does since there are so many things that can go wrong for him, then he's making the heart of Ohio into the biggest potential bomb site you ever imagined."

"That sounds like just a lot of silly talk," Arthur said, and managed not to glance toward Huff, the king of conspiracy nuts when he said it.

"Not so. Add Paul's disappearance and what happened to you at the airport into the mix," Poppy said.

"And I've been in there, all the way to Bunker F," Frank said. "I've seen the stuff, easily enough for two warheads. It's not the sort of thing you can move quickly or move far. I nearly got caught and had to run before I could take pictures or get any documentation. That makes me a liability to Steve. If you don't believe what I saw, believe the racket you heard from Huff's radiation detector and the guys you saw chasing me through the airport."

Arthur paused and scanned their faces before he trusted himself to speak. "How do I fit in whatever agenda you guys have planned?"

If this had been some thriller Arthur had plotted he would have had a hard time arguing the plot he had seen so far past his agent or publisher. But he had followed enough of the newspaper stories to know they essentially had their facts about Steve right. Arthur remembered him as arrogant back in high school, a rich rebel, a win-at-all-costs person even then. His intensity was legend, though he let his bully pal Rolly Stanton do his heavy work for him even then, and Rolly had been an unbeaten golden gloves boxer. Arthur wore a swollen eye for the better part of a week once in testimony to that. Steve thought Arthur had been trying to sneak Poppy away from him, when, in fact, she had been asking what she could do to keep from losing him. Steve had turned Rolly loose on Arthur, who was lucky all he got was a black eye. Irony wasn't lost on him even back then.

"Agenda? You think this is something you have a choice about? From the time your finger left the trigger back at the airport you were in, like it or not," Frankie said. "You've crossed the Rubicon."

"More like Rubicon's cube," Huff said.

The others all frowned at him.

"Cut him some slack," Rod said. "You kinda brush aside, Frankie, it was your ass he was saving."

Huff's voice went up an excited octave. "You realize where we are. Say we go to NEST—the Nuclear Emergency Support Team. They say, 'We know about the Russian highly-enriched uranium. Unitalon's just turning it into low-enriched uranium the way they're supposed to. We're busy keeping our eye on the Al Qaeda and places like Pakistan, Sri Lanka, Somalia.' You see, all the radiation detectors surrounding this country, and the ones the U.S. sent overseas to ports and border crossings, all point outward. The idea that a monstrous threat is already deep inside the states is preposterous. The internal agencies are too busy responding to more than a thousand alarms a day from our own radiation sensors. We need hard proof, and a way to share it." He looked like he had more he wanted to say, but Poppy held up a hand and his mouth snapped closed.

"Putting aside that you've made your living telling lies, on more than one level, you do have a doctorate and your work is respected, to the extent bestsellers can be, so you have credibility," Poppy said to Arthur. "There's an opportunity here for you to do some good with words, to not only get yourself out of a fix but to share the truth for a change."

Arthur sighed. He turned to Huff. "Can you patch a phone line to the outside, one that can't be traced back here?"

"Sure. I could bounce it through enough satellites and . . ."

"Spare us the detail and just do it. Can you set it up on speaker phone and then find the number of the nearest FBI office? I believe it's in Cincinnati."

"Don't even have to look that up," Huff said. "Got it here on file." He shambled over to one of the computer keyboards and began tapping away. In less than five minutes, he nodded to Arthur. They could hear a phone ringing. It came through loud over the room's speakers.

When a receptionist answered, Arthur said, "This is Aris Aaron. I'd like to speak to . . ."

Before he could finish she said, "Hold please. I'll patch you through." That meant he was out in the field somewhere, probably closer than Arthur liked to think about.

In seconds an angry voice boomed at them. "Special Agent in Charge, Gerald Benton here. You're Arthur Sanderson and I think you know why we need to speak to you, *right now*."

Huff gave a smug nod. So much for Arthur's long guarded secret identity.

"I need to tell you about a threat to Ohio's nuclear plants."

"Just come in. We want to hear all about it, and we want to talk to you, face-to-face. Where are you now?"

Arthur could imagine them scrambling on the trace. He hoped Huff's ability to block a trace was as good as the others believed.

"Can we just discuss this by phone?"

"No. You need to come in. *Now*. Make it easy on yourself."

Arthur pressed the button to end the conversation. "You see how it is?" he said to the others.

"I was afraid we might be barking up the wrong tree there," Frankie said. "His credibility isn't all that hot at the federal level."

"What do you mean?" Poppy said.

"I didn't know he was Aris Aaron until you told me, although it appears the Bu has figured that out. But I do know that the famous thriller writer Aris wrote some letters to a Senator that didn't set well. Some Afghani rebels offered to sell thirty or forty Stinger missiles to the U.S. along with a deal that would set one of their own free. The CIA turned the deal down and Aris, or Arthur here, got wind of it through his contact, a retired CIA operative who he'd gone to college with, one of the sources for his thriller novels."

"I heard about that," Huff said, not the best support Arthur could have wished for. "That really happened."

"I sent those letters because not to do so would entail possible prison for me," Arthur said.

"Letters?" Poppy asked.

"Yeah," Frankie nodded, and tried not to grin. "He also shared information from his deep cover contacts about the Pan Am 103 tragedy. He said it resulted from a CIA and DEA drug pipeline operating out of Nicosia and Beirut into the U.S. Yet the witness who testified to congress disappeared. Aris Aaron said that the CIA agent who had participated in the pipeline was the one who took the witness out—all this from his contacts, but with no hard proof."

"You were in Nicosia and Beirut, Frankie," Huff said. "We found that out while trying to find where to reach you."

"You should have kept your nose to yourself. Reunion committee, my ass. But don't miss the point here. We're talking about Arthur's credibility. The feds think he's a nut case, no matter how his books sell. He even wrote them about Operation Rushmore, a CIA/Mossad plot to assassinate then presidential candidate Bill Clinton."

"That really happened too," Huff said. "Arthur wasn't wrong about that. It just got covered up, by guys like you."

"That's okay, Huff," Poppy said. "I see what Frank's saying. Maybe Arthur isn't the right voice to tell the world. Right now he's also a fugitive from justice, not the best status either. But he still is more or less constrained to help clear his own name."

Frank wouldn't leave it alone. He spun to Arthur and pointed a finger at his face. "You had a hard on for the CIA because you were held and questioned . . ."

"For three weeks."

" . . . while your mother died and was buried."

"Do you think I should feel good about that, Frank?"

The look Poppy gave Frank wasn't far from the one Huff had given him earlier, like he was something scraped off the bottom of a shoe. But Arthur didn't care. He nodded toward the flickering television screens. "I just want to do what I can to get out of this mess," he said.

"I don't know if that's possible. I doubt if there's freedom or redemption for any of us," Poppy sighed. "But if we can pull the curtain away from what Steve has up his sleeve we might just save millions of lives. Frank's working with us, for the moment, even though I know how some of us, yourself included, may feel about him."

Whatever she saw on Arthur's face may have revealed long buried feelings, hopes he had had about Poppy even when he was her platonic pal back at school. Thinking that way at all suddenly struck him as more silly and futile than ever, especially in light of the sticky mess he was in. As those icy eyes picked up far more than he wish he'd shared, her lip twisting into its trademark curl as she stuffed his stuff, money and all, back into the bags.

"I hope you'll think hard about being even a reluctant member of the team," Poppy said. She picked up his two bags and brought them over and dropped them on the bed beside him. "You know, I've always had a soft spot for a man who wasn't afraid to run up the pirate flag and get a little dirt on his hands by running amuck. I think you know why you never fit into that role." She stared down at him. "Passport won't do you much good if you try to leave the country anyway, don't you know."

"Gee thanks," Arthur muttered, looking up from the bags into her icy eyes. "You do have some surprises up your sleeve."

She saw something in the way Arthur looked at her. There must have been some of that hang-dog, hurt puppy look he had years ago when he knew she was out of his reach then. The corner of her mouth tugged up. "You picked a funny time to feel frisky."

"I've been jarred out of my socks. That's all."

"Guys. Guys. Focus." Rod said. He stared at Arthur. "I hope you *will* to help us. Don't make Paul's death for nothing."

"Arthur doesn't *have* to do anything," Poppy said, "although his choices aren't what they once were."

"We really could use you," Huff said, "although I wouldn't have wished anyone into the spot you're in."

"The jury's still out if he even has anything in him that can help us," Poppy said.

"It's not out as far as I'm concerned," Frankie said, and he looked right at Arthur.

Frank's eyes narrowed into the squint of a snake. Arthur stared back at him without a flinch of remorse or as much fear as Frank would have liked. Not much brotherly love, either.

Frank moved close, so close the others couldn't hear. "You think you're a clever fellow, don't you? Been to college, learned some Greek, can think like a chess match and fancy that you have all the edge you need for life. Well, let me tell you, you are in way over your head here. This kind of thing spits out your type like used match sticks. So what exactly is up your craw at this point?"

"Things seem too simple," Arthur said. "I'd have made the woman bent, maybe tangled them all up in a conspiracy. I sure wouldn't have just said the goods are in Bunker F, that all you have to do is find and prove that and the whole jig is up."

Frank rocked back a half step, then leaned back into Arthur, who didn't give up any space. "I think you might just get your wish, that all this is a lot more complex and tangled than your smug ass thinks. We'll see how you roll then."

*   *   *

Huff's house grew quiet in the night. He had left a night light on so no one would stumble if they needed to get up in the night. Arthur lay awake listening to every tick and creak and breathing of the others. He had the lower bunk and Rod agreed to use the upper, which meant Arthur could look up and see the cross-hatch of wires that supported the mattress strain in a downward dip, giving him opportunity to contemplate being crushed in the night by a former professional football player. Sweet. That and being surrounded by the close proximity of other people after a life spent living alone.

"The years have been kinder to some of us than others," Poppy had told him. He held up his hands and looked at them in the dim light, could make out the patina of age just beginning to show—tiny waves of wrinkles barely beneath the surface of tiring skin. He could reach and feel pudgy flesh along the waistline that spoke of years of living too well. In the mirror he could see lines around his eyes that were not all from laughing. Sure, inside his mind he was still somewhere around sixteen, young and full of beans, perhaps still a little naïve in a place or two. Yet the body fails to keep stride with that and goes its own way until you seek to do something brisk and it lets you down, or slows you. If he felt that way, he wondered how Frankie rolled with that, a highly trained fighting machine facing the same wrinkles, foibles of the body, yet the sense of having the same keen mind. Maybe that was an illusion as well. And Poppy, who had said she felt eighteen in her mind, did she have the same urges as then, biological and otherwise? What did they all want? He knew for his part he just wanted to be out of this mess and things to be the way they had been. Well, maybe he'd had more than a wishful thought or two about Poppy too. Fat lot of good wishing that did. He conjured a vision of a smoking black hole in the woods where his home had stood. Frankie? Hard to tell what he wanted. Huff probably wanted to be left alone, or maybe just a touch more connected. We could all want that. Poppy, now Poppy. He knew what she wanted, really wanted now—to see Steve Hamilton naked, humiliated, turning slowing on a spit over an open fire. It was not a funny picture, but Arthur almost chuckled as he felt himself drift off to sleep.

Chapter Ten

Poppy came out the front door of Huff's place onto the porch, stepped around Frankie, who was stretched out doing sit-ups, and walked across the clearing toward Arthur using long, graceful strides like some big cat. A leopard, he'd say. He had forgotten how she always walked that way, not ramrod stiff, but upright, like some elegant and poised model in heels on a runway. Back in her cheerleading days she could spring in the air and land in the splits while giving a yell that could rattle rafters. She could equally well whistle like a longshoreman. Yet she always carried a certain quiet dignity about her. The stark contrast, the soft skin, yet firm-flesh aliveness of her used to make Arthur feel like some two-dimensional cartoon character, a sensation he could still feel in flashes.

She came up and stood beside him without speaking. Frankie, bare-chested, huffed away at his workout. No one should be that lean and fit. He'd done over fifty sit-ups already. Arthur could barely imagine him as the pudgy kid he had once known. Sweat glistened on Frank's taut, hard body. Arthur looked away and up into the tree tops at a restless rattle of a couple of dried leaves that hadn't dropped in the fall.

The sun filtering through the trees grew brighter and the

wind picked up and rustled the top budding ends of the tallest of the oaks and beeches even harder. Across the clearing, past an extended-fork motorcycle with sidecar, a clutch of animals, Scrappy the belligerent raccoon among them, gathered close to Huff as he handed out food. They got along better than Arthur expected. The deer crowded close and a mother possum and her little ones waddled out from under a log and headed for the feed, as if to prove to Arthur that they were not just night creatures. Before Arthur could begin humming the tune to "Peace on Earth, Good Will to Men," Scrappy decided to square off just then like some furry little Suma wrestler against the mama possum, who took a stance that said she wasn't going to take any guff from the likes of him, and a flurry of noise broke out. Huff had to wade in, bravely Arthur thought, and sort out the combatants. Huff stood erect at last holding Scrappy by the scruff and the hubbub quieted down. He glanced over to Arthur, looked hesitant, but Poppy gave a head shake and he stayed at what he was doing. Arthur had been right with his earlier observation that all of the others deferred to her, that she was the one in charge here.

"Huff and his peers," Poppy said at last.

"I believe he does relate better to animals than to people."

"This is one hermit critiquing the style and manners of another? You did notice how similar your two hermit retreats are."

Arthur turned to look at her. "Except I don't *have* mine anymore." Oh, he could get to grumpy after all with the right prodding.

"What are you doing out here, soaking up what you think might be a final morning?" she asked.

"Nothing as dramatic as that." Up close, it was hard for him to ignore Poppy. Those hips that moved in silky harmony and with those piercing eyes that missed nothing. He reminded himself she wasn't the Poppy of his adolescence, but stood now an intelligent force all her own, and from what he had seen so far a quite independent woman able to take care of herself—one who didn't need him, didn't want him.

She caught him looking at her differently. "What?"

"I guess I was checking to see if you'd slipped off your bra and had come in to seduce me, if that's what you think it'd take to get me on board."

"That's rich, though my boobs *are* still in pretty good shape for my age. It makes all the difference to not be top-heavy like Candy or some of the other girls back in the day. But no, I didn't shed the bra to reel you in. Would that have worked? Calmed your jets?" She tilted her head, kept after him. "Now really, what are you stewing about?"

"I was just wondering about how much of this is about you wanting to get back at Steve Hamilton."

"And here I was worrying that you were stuck on thinking about possible consequences for yourself."

"Like prison, or death?"

"Yeah, like that." She took a step closer, and such was her presence he nearly took a step back. "Get over it. We all die sometime."

"That's pretty cavalier of you."

"Oh, come on. You were the one who used to tell me how you never wanted to live until you were old. Thirty-five was the age you set back then. You said you couldn't picture yourself sitting around in some rest home in dirty underwear eating hot dogs and ketchup off a paper plate."

"Well, now that I've made it past that, and will be knocking on the door of sixty before long, do you think I ought to move it again?"

"The point is, if you really believe your life should be lived in a burst of flame instead of a gradually dwindling ember, this might be your chance."

"Do you suppose that's the sort of pitch they give the suicide terrorists?"

"Tell me what you *want*, what would make this work for you."

"I might ask for the same thing I suspect you're already giving Frankie."

"And I wouldn't refuse you—if that's what you really needed. Though I suspect it's not."

He looked hard at her. She had been a beautiful girl but was far more striking as a mature woman. There remained the clues of her sprightliness, athleticism, and something more indefinable that had always cast a magnetic aurora, though not one apparently strong enough to keep Steve in tow. Arthur thought again how inside his own head he still felt like the same sixteen or seventeen year old he had been back then. It's a shame when the body can't quite keep up with that sort of thinking.

He sighed. "I used to think I knew what it would take to

make me feel happy, or fulfilled. Maybe spending too many years in a routine with a growing comfort zone took some of that away. I was content with just breathing, getting by."

"What are you saying?"

When he didn't respond, she turned him with a hand on each shoulder so he had to stare into the ice of those eyes. "Look. I'm old enough to know when gravity is just about to start dealing from the bottom of the deck. If you ever really wanted to make any kind of leap to be with me, and I mean *be with me*, you would have to get together enough sand to make that leap. Have you thought it all the way through, what that means, the daily contact, even being a part of the lives of my grandkids, the whole commitment ball of sticky wax?"

"Are those the terms Frankie plays by?"

"Frankie's different from you. Night and day different. He's fling, where you're a pair of boots that would be fitted for life. Is that what you think you really want? Think hard."

Arthur *had* thought about it while on the porch rocker alone at night listening to the wind through the leaves. He'd thought about it alone in his bed, too restless to sleep, facing the solitary rest of his life. He'd even thought about it when exploring the fears that it wasn't commitment he feared, but that of hurting someone by disappointing them, or making the person angry. By person, he meant Poppy, because it had always been her he had pictured during the tossing and turning. He'd seen movies that he had thought were just plain soapy where the man says, "I can't picture living a life without you in it." He'd laughed, but all the soap washed away when he pictured Poppy in that context. Then he felt like he'd been kicked in the stomach by a fairly large mule.

She shook her head and frowned at him. "You're so stubborn."

"That's not fair," he said. "I'm like a sparrow with a hurt wing, and you keep shouting, 'Fly, damn you, fly!'"

"Oh, pul-eeze. You write about characters, and I've noticed you're careful enough to give every one of them a flaw or two. People accept each other in spite of flaws, are maybe even attracted to the odd crippled sparrow. Look at Frankie. Don't you recall how he was when we were young, the unwarranted smugness of someone who looked a second cousin to the Pillsbury dough boy? Can you see him how he was then and how he's managed to evolve?"

"What do you see in him?"

"For one, he's fearless, laughs in the face of danger."

"Sometimes I chuckle out loud at it."

"Yeah, from the comfort of your easy chair. Get out of here. You're the kind of person who shoots their arrows from the safety of castles, behind the thick stone walls where there's never really any risk. The heroes you write about are tough and brave enough, but a hangnail in real life would send you scurrying to the hills."

"Are you saying that I can write about conflict on the page but in real life I dodge it at every opportunity?"

"That's exactly what I'm saying. You've been sitting on the bench so long you're farting sawdust, and don't bring up the time you took a pop on the noggin from Rolly Stanton, because you would have avoided that if in any way you could have seen it coming."

"I don't know about that." He swallowed. He thought of the man in the airport, who he had killed, who was dead now and would never breathe again. But he had to admit he would have tried to avoid that too had he been given five more seconds to think.

"You know your Hemingway. Look at Frankie and then at yourself. You have none of Frankie's grace under pressure, maybe never will."

Arthur caught himself looking at his shoes. He looked up. "Maybe it's time for me to relearn everything, and to put more effort in this time." He hesitated, then looked directly into those eyes that were something of a vortex to him. He felt he could fall inside them. They made him dizzy, uncertain, and had let him get off track. "You kind of skipped over the big question. How much of this *is* you wanting to get back at Steve Hamilton?"

"Why would I care about him?"

"He dumped you, at least once, maybe twice."

She half turned away from him, and at first he didn't think she was going to respond. Her hands balled into fists, and when she spoke the first few words were like taking bites out of the air. "It's true that I was stupid enough to go back to him, after all that time, and have an affair that I thought would fulfill me, that would confirm all along that we were meant for each other. But we weren't. He made that clear enough. And yes, I'd like to see something large and sharp broken off deep inside him, but that's not what this is about."

There was so much passion and emotion in her voice that Arthur almost forgot for a moment she was his age. For a glimmer she had been a fiery teen again.

"I know how you feel," he said, which snapped her head toward him.

"No. I doubt if you do. If you possibly can."

"Somewhere past the desire, and lust, you're on fire with deep disappointment and anger. Worse, there's jealousy, the most vicious green-eyed kind with spurs, and utter rejection? Her being rich, and twenty-four years younger than you, was just enough salt in the wound to make you wonder from time to time if you might just do something about it? Then too, there's probably a good dose of driving guilt involving the late Pecky."

She tilted her head and narrowed one eye. "You have a way with words. I believe that perhaps you do get it."

Rod came out the front door of Huff's place tucking in his shirt. Arthur knew Rod had slept soundly and loudly but he didn't look rested. Arthur wasn't used to sleeping much himself, and that always got worse when he was around people—that "up tight" twitchy feeling of being stoked up on too much caffeine—and it didn't look like Rod did well under those conditions either. He yawned like a cave bear being drawn against his will from his cave. Frankie stood up and began to towel off his lean torso. Arthur checked to see if Poppy was looking his way, but she stared off past Huff and his critters.

Rod saw Poppy and Arthur standing together and came

over to them. "We haven't heard from Wally, and we should have by now," he said, not exactly ignoring Arthur but fixed hard on Poppy's face. "His blip is still where he was, but we can't reach him by cell phone, and he was supposed to come back last night with Huff's hardware. I better go that way and check on him. Want to come along, Arthur, or would you rather stay here and lay low?"

"Is it dangerous?" Arthur asked. He guessed he wanted it to kind of be, since a stubborn part of him still wanted to measure up for Poppy.

"My dad died of leukemia at forty-two after working there, if that's what you mean. Then there's what happened to Paul." Rod lost steam as he talked.

"I don't think any of us should go near just now while the place is stirred up like a hornet's nest," Frankie said. He came over to stand beside them. He buttoned up his shirt and stared at Poppy.

"*You* don't have to," she said, "but *someone* should go with Rod. Will you, Arthur?"

"Yeah, I'm in."

He glanced toward Poppy, caught her raised eyebrow. He said, "Why not."

"I'll go too then," Frankie said, "but I don't think it's smart."

Rod shrugged. "Okay with me, but one of you's gotta ride bitch."

That turned out to be Arthur. The Harley was a nice one, but the sidecar put Rod out of the Hell's Angels class. When he caught Arthur looking at the sidecar he said, "That's where Bitsy rides. You know, same girl I dated back in the day. You never asked, but we've been married all these years and are doing fine. Got grandkids, everything."

He towered over Arthur and his was a face that could look menacing, if he let it. His scowl shifted into a reluctant grin. "I'm a sheet metal worker now, by the way. Have been for thirty-one years. Thinking about starting my own construction company some day, though. That's in case you didn't know that too. He held out a hand.

Arthur reached and shook it. It was like the raspy hand of a steel statue. He could imagine Rod ripping sheet metal apart with his hands, if he chose to. Yet there was still the shadow of a grin on his face as he swung a leg over as he mounted the bike and Frank scrambled into the sidecar while Arthur climbed on behind as Rod slipped on the kind of dark sunglasses made famous by Arnold Schwarzenegger. Rod was every bit big enough to pull off the look. He glanced back to Arthur. "You comfy, bitch?"

Arthur mumbled something.

"You aren't homophobic, by any chance, are you?" Rod asked.

He kicked the engine to life and that did away with any response Arthur might or might not have made.

Frankie and Arthur both wore helmets, which hid their faces. The wind only occasionally tugged at Arthur's jacket around Rod's wide frame.

He did not feel good about this, having long ago become jaded about the chances that the justice system was fair and just, on either a local or national level. Riding on the back of a motorcycle, seeing the town through the small window of a helmet visor, he was the opposite of eager and felt swept along in the worst way.

He felt the sort of helpless apprehension you get when being dragged to the principal's office knowing that a long wooden paddle was probably going to be involved in the discussion. As he was dragged down their high school's hall, ear held in a painfully tight grip by a wizened lady gremlin of a math teacher, he recalled thinking that it is no wonder that some kids get the impression the justice system and all the rules of life are twisted to the convenience of others.

In elementary school, a friend, Dickie Shorb, and he had gone up to a tree in the park beside the playground where others had swung on the limbs and broken some of the branches. A third grade teacher found them there and dragged them to the principal, who had made them memorize a poem in dreadful, stiff iambic pentameter about a tree. The poem was by Joyce Kilmer, who Arthur later learned was a man. The principal had been wrong, the teacher wrong, and the justice unfair. The stupid poem stayed stuck in his head yet.

He supposed it was better than a paddling, something that did happen back in those days, although he wasn't to experience that until high school, again for all the wrong reasons.

It was a fluke, really, not his fault at all, caused by being in the wrong place and bound by the code that usually doesn't allow anyone to squeal on another student.

Huff, a friend to animals above humans even back then,

had sat a couple seats in front of him in a math class. In the middle of class Huff took a sock from his pocket, and untied the knot at one end. Inside was a garter snake—a harmless and beautiful creature, one Arthur had admired in the wild since, but hardly the sort of guest to introduce into the atmosphere of concentration required for higher learning.

Huff let it slither from one arm to the other. Then, attracted by the open purse of a girl in the seat just ahead of him, who happened to be Constance King, daughter of Pikeburg's mayor, he reached and dropped the snake into the purse.

All would have been well if the math teacher had not asked the class to take out a pencil. Constance's hand came out of the purse with the snake between her fingers, and when it wriggled she realized it was not a pencil. She screamed, threw the snake into the air, and pandemonium broke out in the class. As the class tried to settle, Arthur looked up and found the teacher standing over him. The fellow beside Arthur, Luther Banks, and he could not control their laughter, even with her shouting at them. They both denied putting the snake in the purse, but neither would rat out the person who did. That was the code then, the one Poppy had violated.

The principal had tried the standard shouting interrogation style on them that would have gotten him laughed off any Perry Mason show, but he showed who had the ultimate authority and power, even if wrong, when he ended the discussion by giving both boys ten brisk whacks each on the tender spot while they bent in turn over the desk. They had been embarrassed by their tears when the teacher took them back to class. But neither of them let Huff down. Arthur never did hear what happened to the snake. He did know that Luther was one of the ones who never made it back from Viet Nam.

Probably just as well. The town they passed through wasn't much to look at now. It's why Steve Hamilton and people like him lived far away. Arthur had been able to ignore things better himself when he had had his hermit's burrow to return to. Now he was a leaf in the wind, and a jittery one at that.

Huff had said the patrols had dropped, although there was still an "all points" bulletin out on Arthur. There still had been no mention of Frankie on any of the news stations. Even the airport security cameras had failed to point to him, though write some of that off to his knowing what to look for and old habits of staying out of the way of camera lenses. Still, Arthur tensed up the first time they passed a sheriff's department cruiser out on the highway. But they barely caught a glance from the deputies.

They saw a couple more cruisers as they passed right through Pikeburg on their way toward the plant, but these were town cops and seemed bent on missions other than looking for Arthur. One deputy gave Rod a brief wave before turning a corner. That was Dennis McBride, another member of their class who had been part the sheriff's department for over twenty-five years, yet still hadn't made sergeant. He had made the decision to become some kind of cop when his folks were killed by a drunk driver. Arthur didn't know how satisfying that had been for Dennis through the subsequent years. While he had stayed too lean to inspire any doughnut jokes, Arthur suspected he was going to retire eventually at his current rank. A nice enough fellow, who seemed no sharper than a medium-sized marble. Yet, of the department members Arthur knew, he was one of the brainier ones. Given Arthur's current status as a fugitive, that offered small comfort. Whether the local law was bright or not, his ass was still hanging out.

He breathed easier when they headed out the other end of town. A few miles away from the plant, Rod turned up a gravel and dirt farm lane and pulled his bike off into a copse of low bushes that would hide it well enough from the road. He took off his sunglasses and wiped a couple of bugs off them with the thumb of his glove. "We'll have to hike from here."

Frankie didn't say anything, so Arthur figured he had come in this way before too.

Arthur handed the helmet he took off to Rod, who put it in the sidecar beside the helmet Frankie had worn. While bent over, like the lineman he'd been when about to charge into an opposing team, he tilted his head toward Frankie. "Did you do a lot of things you're not proud of?" There was something in his tone, a lack of respect, akin to the looks Huff had been giving Frankie.

"I did things that some wanted done and no one else would do or could do. It's not something you can feel proud or otherwise about." Frankie's mouth formed the fine line Arthur was getting used to seeing.

"Huff said you didn't exactly leave your job as an agent on your own decision. Something went south and you had to cut out. He said they came after you."

Frankie didn't respond, just looked ahead with an impatient squint.

"I refuse to believe," Rod said, "that I live in a country that would flush away its own people when they've done nothing to deserve it."

"I didn't say I'd done nothing," Frankie said, which stopped the conversation.

They hiked in quiet for a couple of miles, over hills and along a stand of trees along a creek before they finally paused. Rod took a careful look about and was about to press on when Frankie spoke.

"Have you ever made a mistake? I did. It was a human enough error and I was new on the job. Years went by and I didn't think it mattered. However—it did."

Rod and Arthur looked at each other, but neither had anything to add to that. When Rod turned and walked on, they followed.

The soil in spring is rich and black in Ohio and each step sank in a half inch. Soon plants would be thick, enriched by the nutriments in this dark ground. It was hard to believe radioactive toxins were probably thicker in it the closer they got to the plant. Arthur wished there was some person or agency he *could* call, someone he could trust to tell his side of the story. It's a hell of thing when you can't trust your own government. But that government had done some blatantly muddleheaded things in the name of the greater good, and a life here and there didn't seem to matter a whole lot.

Arthur was mulling this over and nearly walked into Rod, who had stopped. Rod looked across a ravine to the top of a hill that faced out over a corner of the plant. From there you could see vehicles coming or going, night or day at the plant.

"He's not there."

"I don't like this," Frankie said.

Arthur had to think for a second. "Wally? You don't suppose . . ."

It was as far as he got. The sparse bushes on the other hill parted and six men in black came rushing out toward them.

Rod spun and pancaked Arthur to the ground. He had to be between three and four-hundred pounds these days, and it was still mostly muscle. Arthur didn't have enough air in his lungs to complain. Shots ripped a row of leaves and bark off a Shag-bark Hickory above them. The bits fluttered to fall around Arthur's squashed face. From beside them he heard Frankie squeeze off a couple of slow, careful shots.

"What should we do?" Rod said.

"If I were you I'd run. Run like hell," Frankie said. He fired again.

Rod scooped Arthur to his feet and dragged him along as Arthur struggled to catch his breath and keep up. Behind them the shooting picked up in earnest, and ahead a flash hit the ground and erupted where a grenade from a launcher landed. Rod veered and ran in zig zags through the stark tree trunks. He may have had a knee operation or two, but there is nothing like bullets buzzing past their heads like bees to inspire the kind of speed he'd had as a teen. As soon as he saw Arthur could breathe he dropped him and Arthur was off to the races beside him.

It would take a moment or two for them to get down the ravine and up the other side, so Frankie fired once more and then tucked his gun away and ran. He soon passed them. The three of them ran hard, as if there'd be no tomorrow, and maybe they were right.

Chapter Eleven

Steve tilted back in his Herman Miller Aeron office chair, the kind he had insisted on for all his field site offices. Still, the room around him felt as unfamiliar as a first night in a hotel, though he'd been here often enough. He no longer thought of Ohio as the place he lived, but rather as the place he had to go to when there was a problem.

"What's going on out there, Rolly? There's been some shooting going on. Right?"

Rolly nodded and moved away from where there should have been a window. Instead a wide steel-framed mirror filled most of that wall. Even if they could see outside, the view would reveal only cement and sky.

"Why are we here if there's nothing we can do ourselves?" Steve had a file open on the desk but didn't even bother with the façade of looking at it.

"We're not here to do something just now. We're here in case we need to shift to a Plan B. We're absolutely that close to the edge. Then it's something we will need to do ourselves. I explained all this in the plane."

Steve glanced around the room that was meant to be protective, but felt inhibitive instead. Being inside the windowless office felt like running an aircraft carrier blind while commanding from the bridge. The retaining wall outside would have kept them from having to look at suspicious fetid pools that some people claimed glowed in the dark, and at the thousands of 14-ton rusting metal cylinders of waste that littered the nearly four-thousand acre complex. No matter how much soil was turned over or replaced, small puddles eased back and crews in safe suits swept through the area each morning to see what they could do. That was one reason for the concrete bunkers, to buffer the office from arsenic, mercury, polychlorinated biphenyls (PCBs), trichloroethylene, asbestos, beryllium and who knew what else besides the usual amounts of radiation contamination. Steve felt glad not to have been here back when the workers had been encouraged to do clean up with their bare hands and without protective suits, or with paper suits when they had those, but that's what had led to all those stupid lawsuits the government was still doing its best to ignore or quickly settle.

At the sidebar, Rolly poured them each a jot of Wild Turkey neither needed nor particularly wanted. He brought Steve's shot glass over and put it on his desk within reach. He knocked his own shot back on the way back to the bar for another.

"You know, Rolly, it seems like just yesterday, though it's been more years than I like to admit, that you would be on leave and fly back to the states on my dime. If wearing a uniform and beret as we strolled across the Princeton campus bothered you, well you sure didn't let on. I'd point to someone who in recent weeks had ticked me off even the slightest degree and you would nod and head that way toward what you liked to refer to back then as "one of those sons-a-bitchin' draft dodgers," forgetting handily that I was doing the same thing to miss the war. A few of those victims sure found creative ways to roll over and show their bellies. The others, who took exception and thought they'd fight back, got a first hand hard-fisted exhibition of the sort of training for war the country was giving its men those days. You had the gangly farm boy big-knuckled build back then of someone who had thrown many a bail of hay into a truck. You'd wade into an opponent with the sudden ruthless blur of a buzz saw and you would never, never let up until the other fellow was down, which in the case of those cream puff Ivy Leaguers who had never lifted anything heavier than a Phi Betta Kappa key, was always. Things were sure simpler back in those days."

"Are you saying I ought to be out there myself leading those men against whatever we're up against. I thought we agreed against that for now."

"Not at all, Rolly. I was in a reminiscing, a sign I'm getting on in years. I always thought of us as the sea anemone and the clown fish. I know that at first you always thought you were the one with the poison, but as the years had rolled by I think we both came to realize that the really poisonous one was me."

"I don't care much for the image of me as the clown fish," Rolly said.

"Oh, hell. Be the damned anemone then, if that floats your boat, Rolly."

Rolly hovered near the bottle on the bar and the cell

phone beside it that did not ring. Steve looked at himself in the big mirror, which at least was forgiving and made his hair look blond and his face free of any sign of age. Forced to wait, in uncharacteristic passive roles, they were not all that damned patient about it.

Steve doubted any of the plant's other employees would even notice a flurry of activity on or around the grounds. Rolly's security crews were constantly staging terrorist response practices as all 103 nuclear plants in the U.S. did since 9/11 to keep on their toes. He had been assured too that access by air was being closely watched, and was comforted to think that the Indian Point nuclear plant 35 miles from the heart of Manhattan would make a far better target than an aging nuclear plant in Ohio.

Still, that had not been a deterrent to hackers, who in January of 2003 penetrated the firewall of the private network at Ohio's Davis-Bess nuclear power plant. They disabled the plant's safety monitoring system for almost five hours. No safety hazard to the public resulted only because the plant had been inoperable since workers a year before had found a six by five inch hole in the plant's reactor head caused by boric acid eating away seventy pounds of the reactor. The slammer worm the hackers used had first made its way into an unsecured network of a contractor doing work at the plant. It then wriggled through a T1 line bridging that network to the nuclear power plant's network. It had created a backdoor past the firewall built to block just such programs. That was far from his greatest source of stress.

He was getting painted into a tighter and tighter corner.

The cost of the American Centrifuge system continued to spiral. Money, *his money*, was pouring into the plant at an alarming rate, a desperate rate. Yet it had to work. *Had to.* It was no longer a matter of success or profit, it was about survival. He had never stumbled once in his life and the thought of failure now made ants crawl in spastic itches up and down his arms. He picked up the shot glass and tossed back the bourbon, then resisted the urge to go to the sidebar and pour another.

"Do you think I pay you too much, Rolly?"

"I doubt you pay me enough." He hesitated. "Everything's always about money with you, isn't it?"

"Always has been. I see no reason to change now."

They laughed, but Steve could see that Rolly knew as well as he did that it did not come from their bellies and never made it to their eyes.

Chapter Twelve

Arthur's mother was buried up on a hill under a mulberry tree in a real nice plot left to her by his grandmother's side of the family. The view from there looks over the valley where the town is nestled. If it is possible for people to spin in their grave, he suspected she was doing so at the moment, while laughing all the time hysterically. All his life she had nudged and prodded at him to get more involved and be less stand-offish. She knew the secret of his writing success, but would have perhaps thought of him better if he had just given her two or three grandchildren, if he would have gone Christmas caroling, joined the Rotary Club, or be in any way less of a non-involved recluse. Sure, he sent money off to Doctors Without Borders and half a dozen other charities where he thought he could do some small good. But how much time had he spent immersed in the cares or the issues of the world?

Running as fast as he could, with bullets peppering the bushes and trees around them, he would have laughed himself now if he could catch his breath. Frankie led the rest of them by a good stretch, the advantages of a better fitness regime. The deep ravine of a creek to their right cut them off in that direction. Frank slid to a halt, looked down, hesitated, then jumped off into the air. Rod, who was making pretty good time himself for a three-hundred-plus-pound guy with a supposedly bum knee from his pro football days, got there ahead of Arthur and went through the same motions before he too disappeared over the cliff.

Arthur puffed up to the spot, glanced back and couldn't see any of the pursuers for the moment, then heard a hiss and something plopped by his foot. The end of a black climbing rope lay across one of his hiking boots. Below him, water fell from just to his right over the edge of the cliff in a roar that made two or three bounces before the falls splashed into the wide pool below. The fall was about three or four stories. "Grab it and jump," the voice came from below him.

He saw a glimmer of a face and a wave of an arm. Behind him he heard rustling steps rushing up the hill. He picked up the end of the rope, looped it around his right forearm a couple of times and jumped. Everything happened fast and slow at the same time, like being in a car wreck. He fell out across the tumbling water of the falls, the rope snapped taut and he swung directly toward the water, braced himself by closing his eyes tight. He swung wetly through and several arms grabbed him on the other side.

He blinked his eyes open. The only light came through the tumbling water. Wally Moon stood beside him with a finger held up to his lips, winking one almond-shaped eye. When both were open, he had one eye that was wayward, pointed off in a slightly different direction. Arthur had learned, in the years of growing up with him in a lot of his classes, like gym, not to look off in the direction Wally's other eye pointed to see what it was seeing. Frankie stood behind Wally, wiping droplets of water off his own clothes. Rod had to bend to keep his head from hitting the rock ceiling of the cave. Wally stepped around Arthur and slid a cloth across the entrance of the cave until it was even dimmer inside. He leaned close to Arthur, once he had the covering cloth closed and taped into place to his satisfaction, and whispered into his ear. "From outside it'll look like part of the rock behind the falls."

It wasn't much of a cave, more of an indentation into the rock behind the falls. They were stacked in there like a deck of cards, Frankie with his back to the narrowing back of the hole, Rod bent over, and Wally pressed almost into Arthur. The rock camouflage curtain was the only thing between them and the falls, a drop, and guys swarming down the sides of the hills to where the falls emptied out into a pool.

Arthur stood close to a tiny crack along one side. He could have pulled it closed, but he wanted to see what was going on, though a sudden burst of bullets headed their way would not surprise him. Through gaps in the falls that screened them Arthur could see them more clearly than he would have liked. The men after them worked in efficient quiet, using curt hand signals. They wore dark, like a SWAT team, but Arthur doubted they were official law enforcement, though they knew what they were doing. They checked along the edges of the pool and started to follow the stream on down the slope and around through the trees. Soon they were out of sight. Arthur heard Wally let out his breath for the first time.

"They won't find any sign of us coming out downstream and may come back this way with dogs," Rod whispered.

"They found where I was staked out," Wally still breathed in irregular gasps. "I'd dirt biked in, but they got that, camera, tripod, cell phone, everything. I had the camo sheet and rope on my back in my pack when I ran. Lucky I knew about this place."

"Yeah, lucky," Arthur said.

"Good thing you knew we were coming or we'd be three damned surprised corpses laying out in the woods," Rod said. "Is the stash of warhead uranium still there?"

"Yep. Still in Bunker F where Paul saw it. I used Huff's little nanoscouts. Got the images recorded in a laptop." He patted his backpack in a loving way that told Arthur that Wally was a disciple to Huff's techno leanings.

"What do you mean nanoscouts?" Arthur said.

"You see, Huff learned that the Israelis are making these hornet-sized flying robots they can use to gather information without risk to humans. Huff spent a lot of time on it, and although his aren't as small as that—his are about the size of a small bird—they do work. They aren't perfectly silent either. I think they were spotted and followed back to me. I saved them, though, and have the images they recorded on the computer. But now these guys are after us and I'll bet they come back this way when they don't find us down river. What do you think we should do?"

"I'd vote on getting away from here as soon as it gets darker if they're still downstream," Arthur said.

"That's the first sensible thing anyone's said in a while," Frankie said. "I think that if you three are done playing junior g-men for Huff that we ought to all of us slink out of these woods as fast as we can when the time is right and not come back, ever."

Even with the cool water of the falls pouring past in a noisy gush outside the inside of the cave was warming with all of them crowded in and breathing. No one said anything else for a few ticks.

"What are you saying?" Wally finally managed.

"That Paul is almost certainly dead out here and tucked away where no one's going to find him in a thousand years and that you dick-for-brains are about a half a step behind him."

"Don't you dare talk about Paul like that," Rod said, much louder than the others had whispered.

Frankie waved him silent, but Rod wasn't having any of it. He leaned closer to tower over Frankie. He did lower his voice back to a harsh whisper. "There's no reason to say anything bad about Paul. Got it?"

"Okay. Okay." Frankie gave him a dismissive flick of a hand and turned to Wally.

"I mean it," Rod rumbled. "Say you're sorry."

Frankie spun and Arthur expected him to back away when Rod stepped forward and leaned his head down until their faces nearly touched.

They either make you brave or stupid in the CIA,

because Frankie did not flinch.

"You want to get bent out of shape, Rod, you do it about something that still matters," Frankie said between clenched teeth, "not someone who is as dead as you can get and can't help us one bit. Okay?"

Rod blinked and lifted his head. He seemed as surprised as the others that Frankie had not backed down.

Frankie turned his back to Rod.

They waited for hours, in silence, standing or crouching. There wasn't enough room for them all to sit at once, and bending had to be living hell for Rod. Wally and Arthur both tried to sink into a squat at the same time, bumped into each other, so Wally went first and Arthur squatted down with his back to the wall scrunched in tight beside him, a position only slightly less uncomfortable than standing.

"No spooning, you guys," Frankie said.

Rod chuckled. Wally sighed.

The shadows outside were growing long and the light all around them faded until it was all the way dark in a few minutes.

Arthur hadn't thought of Wally in a long time, and when he did it was with the embarrassed regret that he hadn't gone out of his way to be a little nicer back then. Wally was the kind of kid likely to show up with an onion sandwich in his lunch bag. He wore clothes that looked passed down from an older brother when he didn't have an older brother. The most memorable moment, though, had fixed in Arthur's mind from their freshman year. He and

Wally had sat near the back of a classroom. Wally raised his hand and the teacher called on him. Wally froze. His eyes squinted shut and his nostrils flared and he sat there as still as the cannon on the courthouse lawn. The teacher had moved on. Arthur thought little more about it until the class got up to leave and Wally hung back, stayed in his seat. When he did get up he shot for the door. Arthur passed by Wally's desk and there was a puddle on the seat.

Funny how that went. One small moment. A tiny ripple in a tiny pond. The thing was, that was the only single moment he could clearly recall about Wally for all their high school years. There should have been more, a touch more fabric to hold them closer. He was surprised that Wally hadn't been one of the ones to move away, but he had stayed in the area all these years. His eye kept him 4F when others in the class were being fitted with uniforms. It didn't seem fair to Wally's memory that the single moment Arthur recalled with greatest clarity was one of a number Wally had probably struggled to forget through the years. Still, it had been a darn good thing he had stayed around. He had sure enough saved their bacon when those Unitalon men were after them.

In the dark, Wally leaned closer until his mouth was an inch from Arthur's ear. He whispered as softly as he could. "The way it started will make a good story someday, if I ever get to tell it."

Arthur didn't dare turn his head and try to answer. He was as captive an audience as there ever is.

"I was driving along," Wally whispered, "trying not to think about heading toward a ten hour shift behind the counter of the Gas & Go, when the car ahead of me veered off the road, crossed the gravel shoulder and drove right down a slope and into a tree. I thought, 'Can you believe that?' I pulled over and ran down to the car. The woman had a cut above her left eyebrow. Like any scalp wound it bled worse than it looked. She was crying. From the tissues and empty tissue boxes piled on the seat beside her I figured she had been crying for some time. She said to me, 'Just let me die.' I said, 'You aren't hurt that bad. Were you trying for suicide?' She looked up at me and for the first time I realized it was Rod's wife Bitsy. She said, 'I hate my life.' I got her out of the car and she clasped onto me tight as a barnacle. When I tried to ease her down she wouldn't let go. 'You can understand,' she said. 'Mary Kate walked all over you for years before she left you.' I never thought I'd feel good about as ugly and as emasculating a divorce as anyone could ask for."

Arthur tried to wave him quiet, but Wally wasn't having any of it.

Wally whispered on, his breath warm against Arthur's ear, "She quivered and turned her face to me, an attractive and vulnerable woman. Her body was warm and pressed against me. Her lips—*I was thinking I should be calling 911*—the kiss went on for the better part of an hour. The sound of cars stopping along the road gave me the strength to push her away, and I don't know why I said it, but I said, 'I'll try to make it a better life for you,' and I did, even though it had meant some juggling, and some lying, and some sneaking around. But I did it. Our times together, when she wasn't tugged away by the needs of her kids or grandkids, were story book great. It was like being kids again, for both of us, frantic, passionate needy, grasping-each-moment kids. There was just one loose end. Rod."

Wally fell silent and Arthur hoped that was it, and he sat waiting to see if Rod had overheard any of it. But the roar of water from the falls must have masked the confession Arthur could have pretty well done without.

Wally finally spoke out loud to the others. "What's the plan now?"

"You climbed down to this cave, Wally. Then we can climb back up."

Arthur was afraid Frankie was going to say something like that. Wally gave a low groan.

"Just watch yourselves out there and stay away from Hamilton's men."

"I don't know. I might just want to tangle up with them some," Rod said. His deep voice grew louder once again inside the cave and took on the resonance of the late singer Barry White. There was a growing edge to Rod's tone.

"I don't think I want to mess with any of the ones I saw," Arthur said.

"You know something, Arthur," Rod's voice rumbled, "most of the time I'm as sweet as buttermilk, calm as a butter bean. But every once in a while I take a notion to thump something, and I feel one of them moods coming on where Paul's death is concerned."

"Come on. Let's move out," Frank hissed back to them.

"What put you in charge all of a sudden?" Wally said. "Maybe we're safer in here. I'm not sure I want to listen to you, a cashiered or fired antique agent who's maybe still working for Steve. I know I don't want you for our leader, or our hero."

"Right. This coming from someone who pulls a night shift at a convenience store these days. You'd as soon follow the beck and call of that Geek, Huff." Frankie turned to Arthur and Rod. "Is that how you two feel?"

"I don't think any of us is exactly antique," Arthur said. "We're middle aged, or a bit beyond that. Of the lot of us, Frankie is the most fit, and perhaps most used to this sort of activity. But I don't know that we need a leader. We just need to all go in the same direction, and we should probably get going soon."

"I'm okay with that," Rod rumbled. "I just don't want anyone telling me what to do if I decide to take out a little payback for Paul. Got it?"

"Suit yourself," Frankie said. He grabbed the coil of rope from Wally and eased around the edge of the curtain, looked for a handhold, and started up into the thick spray.

Of course, they all had to follow Frankie. He at least secured the rope at the top so all they had to do was use the damn thing to pull themselves back up the wet cliff face. It was a hard climb up the small rope for Arthur, and his hands slipped and burned on the rope a couple of times, but Rod was right behind him and that spurred Arthur on and kept him from slowing. As he neared the top Wally reached down to give him a hand up.

From the top of the cliff they could see moving beams of light in the valley below. The men chasing were coming toward them.

"This way, Frankie hissed, and took off in a run.

"Damn his being in such fit shape," Arthur huffed in a low whisper to Wally. Branches tore at his jacket. A low limb scraped across his forehead. They ran up hills and down into steep valleys, with barely enough light to keep from slamming into trees. They huffed and it seemed like they had been going for nearly an hour. Arthur had a stitch in his low ribs and he could hear Wally gasping like a fish out of water. Rod was way ahead of them, but soon he slowed, then stopped. He looked around.

When Wally and Arthur caught up to him, Rod turned to them and said, "Where do you suppose Frankie has gotten to?"

Chapter Thirteen

The dim light of the rising splinter of a moon clawed its way through the shreds of clouds and swaying tops of sparsely leafed trees to barely light the spot along the path where they had stopped. Arthur heard Wally's loud panting as he sought to get his breathing back to normal. All three stood within arm's length of each other. Arthur would have objected to the proximity to people at any other time, but even after quite a while pressed too close together in the cave he found it comforting now. He listened hard, sought to hear the sounds of those who pursued them, caught just the sound of dried leaves rustling along the forest floor in the night breeze. Nor could he see the beams of their lights sweeping through the trees as they ran this way.

While he could hear Wally's breathing, Rod made no sound. Arthur eased closer, looked up to see wet glistening on Rod's moonlit dark cheeks.

"Rod?" he said. "Are you . . .?"

"He's crying," Wally said. He crowded closer. "What is it, big guy?"

"Nothing." Rod's voice quivered.

For some reason, his response sent the worst kind of chills up Arthur's spine. The one guy of them big enough to break bricks with a snap of his fingers was falling apart on them.

Rod made no noise, but his shoulders shook and his hands balled into tighter fists.

"Rod?"

"Yeah?"

"You okay?"

"You wouldn't understand."

"Give us a try. We need you to be strong right now."

"Well, after all. Bullets against fists," Wally said. "I don't blame him. We *should* be distraught."

"Wally?"

"What?"

"You're not helping." Arthur moved closer to Rod, even though he felt himself tighten inside. Before he could say anything, Rod began to speak.

"There's something I need to tell you guys, to get off my chest. But it can't go any farther."

"Save it, Rod. Don't say anything now you won't be able to take back later. We should be moving."

"Yeah," Wally agreed. "Let's just get away from here."

"I've got to say this."

He whispered, was barely audible above the wind. Arthur glanced around into the dark of the too still woods.

"It's about Paul."

"Paul Felsenfeld?"

"Yeah. It's about him—and me."

"Rod. Don't do this, man," Arthur said.

"I'm not sure what starts this sort of thing. My father, you know, died when I was five. I never really knew him. My stepfather—now him I knew, all too well."

129

Arthur thought he heard the hurried rustling of men off in the woods not far from them. It was painful to strain to catch the least sound and at the same time try not to hear what Rod was saying.

"I was always a giver, and when I quit fooling myself I knew I was at least bisexual. I never told any of you, because, well, you know."

"Rod. I mean it. Stop now, while you can," Arthur whispered.

The rustling grew louder, carried above the wind. Now and then a beam of light swept the tops of the trees.

"I came to know I was happiest only when I'm serving someone else, focusing on making them happy. Bitsy couldn't understand that. It made her crazy. She wanted to make me happy, but with me it was all about her, *doing* for her, *giving* to her. You'd think that would be a good thing for someone with her passion and drive. It wasn't. You see, I have a submissive side, big as I am. She tried. Give her that. But came a time she got tired of never being able to give herself. That stifled her. Who can blame her?"

How Rod could stand there with tears streaming down his face while armed men were rushing through the woods toward them was beyond Arthur's understanding. Yet he kept his mouth shut, like Wally, and let Rod vent, even when he wanted to get a large cork and shove in Rod's pie hole before he shared any graphic details.

"Everything I did only seemed to shut her out, give her no chance to give herself. She—well, we quit spending as much time together. It's like I'd lost interest in her, only I hadn't. There was just no easy way to explain it. I think she began to see someone. I can only hope she did. It's the only way—we were better for a while. For me, there was Paul. And now he's dead. These bastards killed him, and there's nothing I can do about it. Nothing."

"We should get moving, Rod," Wally said. "Please."

"I don't want to run. I want to face them. I want to see the color of their insides."

"They're armed. We're not. It would be senseless," Wally said.

"Shhh," Arthur hissed.

"What?" Wally whispered.

"The noise I'd been hearing coming from over there has gone away. Maybe by standing still they've gone around us."

"Yeah, maybe," Wally said, and as soon as the words were out of his mouth the lights in three beams flipped on in a surrounding circle around them and began moving in closer.

Arthur could make out the shapes of men now. The lights were fastened to the weapons they held.

"Don't do anything crazy, Rod," Wally whispered.

"I'm cool. I'm cool," Rod kept saying in a way that was anything but cool.

Arthur waited for the men to speak. He hoped one would at least call out to tell the others to keep them alive. None of them said a word as they got closer. He could make out faces now. Even in the dark they had streaked their faces with wide black lines like tiger stripes. They did not smile, seemed incapable of smiling. Arthur felt his heart beat faster, like it wanted to climb its way out of his chest. At any moment these men could open fire, and that would be it.

He heard a thump and saw the knife handle suddenly in the man's neck, saw him reach for it and his hand stop midway as he tumbled to his side. The light crumpled out on the man to Arthur's left. He heard the twist and chop on a body. By the time the third man's light swung that direction there was only a crumpled body of the ground to see. A human shape flew out of the air at the man and he twisted, tried to aim his automatic with one hand and reach for his sheathed knife with the other. His back arched and his neck snapped. Frankie dropped lightly to the ground as the man's body fell. He did not even seem to be breathing hard.

"Come on, guys. There's an opening out this way. Let's move. *Now*," Frankie said. He walked across and retrieved his knife from the neck of the first man, wiped its blade on the body before putting it away.

"Holy carumba," Wally said.

"Frankie," Rod said, his voice more raspy than it had been. "I owe you a . . ."

"Save it," Frankie snapped. "Keep quiet. Let's go. Come on now." He started off at a trot.

"Did you hear any of what I said," Rod puffed as they all broke into a run and rushed to keep up this time.

"More than I wanted to," Frankie said. He ran faster. This time they all put everything they had into staying with him.

Chapter Fourteen

"We should have stayed in Bethesda." Steve paced past the desk, past the black leather couch and mahogany coffee table, past the matching wood sidebar where Rolly stood near the half empty bottle of Wild Turkey. The bourbon did not even tempt now. His mind swept through one permutation after another. Outside it was dark now. What was taking them so long? A bunch of clumsy locals, except that damned Frank. Still, they needed a good sweeping up, one and all. Maybe the whole town did.

The shift from being a big shot in a small town at Pikeburg to being just another student at Princeton had opened Steve's eyes. He went there because his father had, and as a major shareholder in Dayton, Power & Light he saw that his legacy son made it in too. Everything had come too easy. There had been Poppy, and Mary Ann, but that had been just going through the motions. At college he had breathed a deeper air of heady challenge. He learned to battle and scrap for what was his. Even the women had demanded that he prove himself to them, like that political activist firebrand Astrid Lazo, though he would not loop back to her until years later when her daddy's oil wells were producing. She had not been an easy conquest, nor had she been easy to shake off when he had gotten all he could from her.

He had read somewhere that Leland Stanford's wife, when the small college her railroad husband has started in California was still a fledgling, had visited Princeton and had seen black squirrels scampering across the college lawns. That, she decided, was what made a quality school, having black squirrels. So she had ordered some and had turned them loose on the Stanford campus.

That's how Steve had felt at first, like some transplanted black squirrel that had been moved to where it neither belonged nor fit. He had dedicated himself to clawing his way into a sense of rightness about being there, which meant negotiating around a few wrong choices of friends and lovers at first, and with Rolly's help, dealing with anyone reluctant to give him respect, or fear. By the time he graduated, he disdained almost every other person on the campus, faculty and students alike, and felt alive for the first time in his life. They all knew damned well who he was. He was destined for greatness, and it was up to him to grab it.

He had never felt uncertain since, until now.

Chapter Fifteen

A dirty rime of pale yellowish light scratched its way up all along the horizon by the time they had rounded up Wally's eleven-year-old green Ford Ranger and had taken the long way around Pikeburg to avoid seeing anyone or having anyone see them.

Arthur rode with Wally, who spoke little except to bemoan again that those goons back there had destroyed the dirt bike he had used to get from the truck closer to the plant. It was the only bike he had, and he'd had it quite a while and went on about it far longer than necessary. Arthur did not push or feel too chatty himself. The vivid picture of Frankie in action kept replaying like an action newsreel loop. Even though it had been in their defense, the detail of snaps and thumps, made with such trained effortlessness, outplayed most of the description of combat in his own thriller books. He felt too dazed to even draft any of this in his head as a novel, although there would be a number of things he would change or do differently if he did. One of them loomed ahead, where the motorcycle was pulled up outside what had been Huff's gate.

The sliding bars had been smashed open and lay crumpled to one side. One stone corner of gate had crumbled and the tall deer fence tilted down at the corner, tired and limp. Smoke rose up above the trees ahead, bringing back an altogether uncomfortable memory for Arthur. It hit him like a punch that Poppy was back there.

Rod fired up his motorcycle and Wally stayed close behind with the truck.

"Faster. Faster, Wally," Arthur shouted. He need not have bothered. Wally had the truck's gas pedal to the floor and fishtailed along the curves of the dirt drive back to the house. Fast as they went, the motorcycle beat them and Frankie and Rod both stood beside it staring as the truck pulled up.

At the clearing, what was left of the house smoldered in the blackened hole of rock that was meant to protect but had failed. The exterior lay crumpled in on what had been the *Architectural Digest* white interior of the living area, while the many televisions of the back room lay in broken smoking shards in a pile.

Arthur waded into the smoldering mess. "Poppy. Poppy. Huff."

"You'd better wait," Frankie called to him. "Knowing Huff, there could be explosives waiting to go off."

"If anything was going to explode, I think it already has," Arthur said. He shouted, "Poppy, do you hear me? Huff?"

Rod waded in beside him, tossing aside the heavier rubble as they pressed on toward the panic room.

"Not good," Frankie said. He and Wally followed in their steps. They all stopped in front of the twisted curl of steel that had been the panic room's door. Crushed cans of tuna lay in a pile that half buried the twisted cot that once was going to be their home for the night.

"Poppy? Huff?" Arthur's voice softened and grew rough at the edges. He looked around, blinked at the destruction.

"Maybe they weren't here. Maybe they got away," Wally said.

Arthur looked at him and got swept away in wherever the wayward eye was trying to point.

"I don't think so," Rod rumbled. "Can you imagine Huff leaving his house? I can't."

"He was a quirky dude," Wally said. "But I always liked him. He may have had his thing about conspiracies, but he was the smartest single person I ever knew."

"His thing about conspiracies may not have been that far off after all," Frankie admitted. "At least this time."

"I didn't know him as well as I should have, but I always respected him," Arthur said. "What about Poppy? Do any of you see anything like a body?"

The singed leaves of an open book on secret societies fluttered with each tug of the breeze.

"Some heavy explosives were used, and they shot the front door lock off," Frankie bent low to look at something. "Looks like they took out the chubby raccoon while they were about it. But I don't see any human blood or bodies. I don't know. I just don't know." Frankie eased and lifted his way through the rubble. He bent to pick up a door, peered under it, then let it drop.

"I'm gonna miss Poppy and Huff," Rod said, his voice again choked with emotion. "They were two wonderful people."

From below a pile of fallen panic room wall a rattle of bent cans preceded a floor-level vault door of steel and concrete swinging to flop open with a soft crash. Huff's tousled graying hair lifted from the slender gap of a space just big enough for one person.

"I appreciate the eulogies, guys. But I'm not quite dead, yet." Smudges of black covered part of his face where white dust had not settled to cake his skin. It gave him a startling zombie appearance.

"Poppy?" Arthur said, louder than he wished.

"They took her," Huff said.

"Your panic room has a panic room?" Wally said, peeking down into the small space from which Huff crawled.

"Who?" Frankie said. "Who took her?"

"I think you know." Huff brushed at the sheet rock dust that covered him.

"Took her?" Arthur said, hating that he sounded like a lousy echo. "Took her where?"

Huff stalked through the house like a dead man. His head moved in jerks as he took in all that was destroyed.

"Are you sure?" Rod said.

"Yeah. I saw them grab her. I heard them mention Rolly Stanton's name, Steve Hamilton's number one man. There was nothing I could do. They were after me next and I heard them setting the charges when they couldn't get in the panic room." He blinked and looked up from the smoldering rubble. "And I know why they took her too."

"Why?" Arthur said.

Huff nodded toward Frankie. "They'll want to trade her, for him."

"Well, it won't do any good to trade," Frankie said. "They'll have to kill the lot of us anyway."

"We're so in over our heads," Wally moaned. "I wish we could just stop and go back the way we were."

"How did they know where to go, to Huff's place?" Arthur said. He glanced around at the faces of the others.

"You think we have a leak?" Frankie said. "Or are they just way more clever than this lot."

Arthur shook his head and looked up to where the smoke was lifting up in a black column. "I wonder if there's any way we can get her back from them, to save her? And I wonder how much time we have before someone spots this smoke?"

"Not as much as you think," Frankie said. He nodded toward the dirt drive. A sheriff's department cruiser moved carefully along the road, easing up to them.

The car slowed, then stopped as if the driver felt either indecisive or was calling for backup. The door swung open and the lone occupant stepped out to pan across each of them through silvered aviator glasses. Go ahead, hitch your gun belt up, Arthur thought. The man reached down and did so. His frame had been stretched into a long and lean model, so that ruled out his spending too much time in doughnut shops. He wore no hat, which allowed the streak of white ran up slightly off center through one eyebrow of otherwise dark hair to make him look oddly dashing or the one eye to look like some lopsided skunk, depending on your bias. Dennis McBride. What were the odds?

Arthur knew that Dennis had come to law enforcement late in life. Being a policeman or deputy sheriff had been a distant dream until his parents were killed by that drunk driver. Going through academy at that age is no walk on the beach, but he drove himself to graduate and took the first opening that came along. He seemed happy in his work, which made everyone suspicious of him, especially the sheriff, who was a dozen years younger and would have preferred just to be given money and not have to work.

Rod started to say something, but Dennis held up a finger to stop him. He reached up to click off a small black box clipped near his collar, thus cutting off his link to headquarters. That made Arthur wonder.

Dennis took off his glasses, folded them, and slid them into a shirt pocket. His eyes narrowed and swept them again. "What's going on here?"

Huff beat the others and said, "As you know, Arthur here is a well-known neat freak and I invited him over to help with the Spring cleaning. You can see the place is a shambles. The others came along to help."

Dennis did not blink once. "Anyone else have a smart ass answer?"

No one spoke. Dennis nodded as if that was just what he expected. He said, "Arthur has an APB out on him, and though you weren't mentioned, Frankie, I know you're trouble. Fact is, I'd heard you were dead. You might just be a pretty fit ghost. Now come on. Someone talk or I turn my communication back on and call this in. That is, if some busybody hasn't seen the smoke and already made the call."

"Are the Bu people stepping on you hard, Dennis?" Arthur asked.

Dennis hesitated. "Yes. Yes they are, and that damned Sheriff Bob has his head so far up that Gerald Benton's butt that he can't see for shit. There's been a Kennedy as Sheriff in this county for three generations so it's hard for the voters to say no to another one. But the public sure got the 'Rain Man' version this time. Plus his head's so far up this Bureau Chief Gerald Benton's butt it's a wonder he can see at all. Benton worries me even more. Seems like we should have had a whole lot more action from the feds by now on this, but he seems to be positioning himself for some sort of limelight. That sort always worries me."

"That's what I thought."

"That's astute of you, Arthur. Where do you get that?"

"The feds think locals are incompetent at best and often more dangerous than helpful to the public. I figure you've had a snootful of them or you'd be wrestling me to earth, slapping on the cuffs, and asking questions later."

"Gosh, I wonder where the feds could pick up that stereotype? Couldn't be by reading the books of Aris Aaron, now, could it? I know he's expressed that view a time or two."

"Um." Arthur glanced to the others.

Dennis looked over his shoulder, then back to them. He did not blink. Something gnawed at him. Arthur held up a hand to encourage the others to let Dennis get it off his chest.

"Let's talk about ambitions. Mine was to be a cop, or deputy, nothing fancy, just that. It's what I've got and I'm happy with it, although I would risk it if the right occasion came along. Now, Gerald "your tax dollars at work" Benton, he has ambition in buckets. I don't know what for, perhaps to be the next J. Edgar Hoover, Eliot Ness, or even president. If you were to tell him he's likely to play out as no higher than Bureau Chief of Cincinnati I doubt he'd believe you. That fire in his belly, whether it has any chance or not, is going to get someone hurt, maybe several someones."

"I think we need to talk about Poppy," Rod said.

"What about her?" Dennis started to lean one forearm on the grip of his sidearm, but caught himself in time.

"I think this is the time we tell you everything we know about what's really going on and see how you feel about it." Rod looked to each of the others in turn.

"I think that would be a good idea," Dennis said.

"I don't."

"No one's asking you, Frankie. You have the floor, Arthur." None of the chairs had survived, so McBride moved over to what was left of a broken couch arm that leaned against a crumbled section of wall and eased himself down onto that.

They were taking a chance one way or the other with their deputy classmate, but he was already here and hadn't scooped them up. What swayed Arthur was Dennis turning off his link to headquarters when he arrived. Arthur debated whether he should only share part of the story or all of it.

He decided that a third or a half would sound phony, so he told everything he knew and some of the things he thought. His tale ended with, "So now Steve has Poppy."

Dennis nodded slowly to himself. "A lot of things make a whole different sense now. You know, by rights, I *should* take you in Arthur."

"I know, Dennis. But little can come of that. I'll be whisked away, and if Steve's clout is what I think it might be I'll be out of the picture entirely."

"That Steve is one clever S.O.B. He's sure got you by the short hairs now." Dennis ran a finger along the side of his chin. "You can't ask for help or Poppy's dead. You probably don't want to give him Frankie, even if Frankie was willing. He isn't I can bet. So you've got to handle this yourselves. What have you got planned?"

"We haven't got as far as a plan yet," Rod said. "We'd be glad for your help, Dennis."

"I should know more after I look at the videos we got of the plant. Those are still safe, aren't they, Wally?" Huff looked that way.

Wally held up the backpack and started toward Huff with it.

"We know you'd be taking a risk. But with Poppy at stake your help could be huge. We can do all we can not to jeopardize your job." Arthur took a deep breath and waited.

"Well," Dennis sighed, "all I can say is that you caught me at a good time. On any other occasion I'd take you in and we'd sort everything out later and the department would handle everything that needs handling. Only kidnapping is federal and Benton and his suits would take everything away from me. The other deputies, under Bob Kennedy's direction, would let him. The man's out to make a reputation and he smells something big and doesn't want any of the locals in his way. So I'll play along for a bit, as long as you're straight with me. But the minute things threaten to get ugly I have to send up the blue flare and bring in the pros from Dover, such as they are. Understood?" He looked into each of their faces. "I'm off shift in an hour and will expect to share everything. Now, let's take a closer look around and see what we can find before the feds toss the area. Then you can talk about what to do next."

They each poked about, Huff looking the saddest at each new destroyed item he found. He wanted to bury the raccoon, but Frankie said they didn't have enough time. When Dennis stood near Arthur for a moment he leaned closer and nodded toward Frankie. "I probably don't need to tell you this," he whispered, "but I wouldn't trust that one any farther than you can throw him."

Chapter Sixteen

"What do you mean they got away and killed three of your best men? Rolly, your men are supposed to make Navy Seals look like puppies, or so you said. What the hell? How'd they get away?"

"We think it was that damned Frank." Rolly stood over by the mirror, glad he could not see outside where it was still black and far from cheerful. "That son of a bitch just became priority number one." He looked around the room for something he could throw, or break.

"You hear that Poppy. Your new boyfriend doesn't know who he's dealing with, or that your life is hanging by a thread. I think he needs a lesson. What do you think?" Steve sat tilted back in the chair behind the desk with his legs up on it, crossed at the ankles.

"I think I have to revise my opinion of you to lower than even I thought possible. I do believe you're dying your hair too. You were never so blond. Well, it's a wonder you aren't bald. Had a tummy tuck too, or have you just denied yourself food?"

Rolly suppressed a chuckle. He had been watching them since he brought her into the room, and, oh yeah there was tension there. He was pleased to see it was all from her end. Steve looked calm and unruffled, which only seemed to get under her skin all the more. Good for him. Poppy reached up to her hair, tried to smooth it into place. Rolly could have told her Steve was far too centered and focused these days to succumb to any attraction or history they might have. He could have told her too that her glare of indignation was not the right card to play either.

"You know, Rolly and his boys checked your place first before we got tipped off where you were."

"Who tipped you off?"

"That damned dog of yours nearly denutted Louis? Louis is one of Rolly's favorite men."

"What did you . . .?"

"I shot at him," Rolly said. "Give him this. He's dodgy, but I think I got him."

"You shot François?"

"I hope to hell I did. It's going to be a long time before Louis has a snappy answer to 'How they hanging?'"

"And you, my dear Poppy, unless you're bulletproof yourself, had better shut the hell up for a while."

"I'll . . ."

Rolly yanked so hard on her arm above the elbow she had to shift her feet to catch her balance, but it shut her up. He tugged her toward the door while he had her moving.

Rolly led her down the long hall to the empty office they could use for a holding cell.

"You know," she said, without a glance his way, which was fine with him, I finally figured out what Steve's real love has always been. Money."

Rolly said nothing, but kept a firm hand on her upper

arm.

"There was me, Mary Ann, then that chili pepper hot Astrid. Mary Ann and Astrid probably never caught on. They'd grown up with too much of the stuff. Steve never had as much as he wanted."

Rolly let her talk.

"Some say that once you have real money it's almost impossible not to make more money. Well, they sure didn't pick the utility field the way Steve did. It may have seemed ripe for the picking, but the fact that even our deep-pocket government was backing away from it as fast as it could should have sent some sort of message. Yet that's just the thing, the kind of on the razor's edge of risky challenge that would have tugged at Steve. I'll bet he's absolutely desperate. He must be a bear to be around."

Aw, let her ramble on. She was just jawing to keep from screaming out loud, though she did come close to a nerve. Still it was a game Steve said they could win. Steve was always the gambler ready to play at the really big table. He had a taste for it and a skill at it. Rolly liked the part where he got to roll up his own sleeves and get busy with his fists. That was business as he knew it. Everyone needs to have one skill or aptitude to draw from if they are to make it. He knew what his own was.

When he was twelve he had a little shaggy-furred five-year-old dachshund he loved named Sasha. To see what he was made of he had called her to him. When she scurried across the carpet, leaped up into his lap and wriggled into place he had squeezed her neck and twisted until those eyes that looked at him in surprise and pain bulged and then faded. He knew then he was capable of anything that was ever asked of him.

He opened the door and nudged Poppy inside. She spun and glared at him. "Whatever you're thinking, I hope you choke on it."

He swung the door shut and turned to go back up the hall, chuckling out loud this time as he went.

*   *   *

Poppy could see a rippled and uncertain version of herself in the reflection of a steel plate that covered the door. The image was hazy and the twist to her mouth looked to her more disappointed than ironic. She wasn't sure why it suddenly seemed so important that she see herself, confirm that it was really her locked in here. She tried the handle. Locked. Worth a try.

Hard to tell what this room had been. There had been shelves once, but they had been removed. This was probably where they held Paul before they . . . well, she didn't like to think about that. Poor François, and Huff. She'd watched them set the charges and poke around in the rubble before they left. Her grief shifted to the raw heat of anger and she kicked at the door. Bad judgment. She only thought she'd been mad before. She limped across the room looking for anything she could use as a weapon. Nothing. Nothing small she could use to pick the lock either, even if she knew how. No windows. The walls weren't sheet rock she could punch through. They were solid painted cement. She choked back a sob. No, she damn well wasn't going to cry. That worthless bastard couldn't bring her to that. Never again.

They'd played right into Steve's hands, and who had nudged them? Worse, someone had leaked where they were staying, at Huff's place. Think.

She paced across the room. Think. She slammed the wall with the flat of her hand. That stung. Why was she still alive? Because Steve wanted something. Frank? Well, she thought hard about that and felt pretty sure that if her getting out this mess alive depended on Frank getting her out of here she was going to have a damn long wait.

Chapter Seventeen

Huff unlocked the padlock to an outdoor storage unit—the kind that come in rows where you can store your stuff if you don't mind the occasional insect or rodent square-dancing across your possessions. Arthur stepped out of the way as Huff swung the door open wide. A black four-wheel-drive Chevy Silverado 2500 pickup truck with an extended cab, this year's model, pulled up beside Wally's green truck and Rod's motorcycle. It sparkled like a black pearl in the sun. Someone had spent a lot of time taking care of this baby. Dennis McBride, in civilian clothes, climbed out of the cab and walked toward them with the confident stroll of a sailor on shore leave. Arthur could make out the bulge of a backup gun strapped to one ankle and guessed a service automatic was shoved in the back of the belt under the light jacket he wore.

"Do you really think it's such a good idea working with a cop on this?" Wally whispered.

"I think it's a great idea. The sides are muddled up enough it's nice to know some authority's on our side." Rod nodded to Dennis as he joined them.

Huff swung the corrugated metal door open and flipped on a light.

Dennis was the first to step inside. "You got a lab in

here?"

"Yeah." Huff carried the backpack over to a counter and took out the laptop, had it hooked up and booted in seconds. "Some of the stuff I mess with needs a little distance from my place. Nothing like meth being made in here, if that's what you mean."

"Holy crap. You've got chemistry stuff and all kinds of electronic connections in here. I thought you'd been wiped out and were out of business." Dennis took a couple more steps inside and looked around at an array of equipment, the kind his department probably couldn't afford.

Arthur took in the life-sized poster of Doctor Who and noted that the hot pads Huff used with his chemistry lab showed the images of Daffy Duck and Bugs Bunny. The mind of a genius is a strange and multi-faceted place indeed.

Huff flicked on a high-resolution nineteen-inch computer screen. The guys crowded around the screen like a holiday football game was showing. Instead they watched a jerking flight video taken by one of the small bird-sized nanoscouts.

"What are we supposed to be looking for?" Rod asked.

"That's Bunker F," Frankie said. "Nothing going on around there except extra guards."

Huff busied himself over on the chemistry side of the room analyzing samples he had taken from the small flying device. He seemed to know what they would see on the video recorded.

"Hey, they see the device. They're after it," Rod shouted.

"Yeah, I had to turn it around and make it scoot. The little sucker can fly." Wally did little to suppress his admiration of Huff's toys. "If the camera was pointed back that way you could see they were shooting at it. I went into evasive maneuvers and got it back. But I barely got away myself and if they hadn't stopped to trash my bike they might have realized how slow I was going. Lucky I knew about the cave."

"What are you doing over there?" Arthur turned away from the screen and watched Huff run the kind of tests that meant little to him, even though he'd paid pretty fair attention most of the time in high school chemistry some forty years ago.

"Did anyone notice anything unusual on the video?" Huff asked.

"The trucks?" Dennis said.

"Exactly."

"What about them?" Wally said.

"Four of them, with 387 Peterbilt day cab tractors without the sleeper unit pulling shiny new Fruehauf trailers. That's the aerodynamic model diesel, by the way. They can really fly."

"What the hell?" Frankie said. "Are you saying what I think you are, Huff?"

"That's right. Steve's Plan B has its own Plan B."

"They're going to try to move the stuff?" Dennis crowded closer. "What do these tests mean that you're running?"

"I'm after air particulates, anything unusual. I'm getting

a high score on lead, and on paint."

"Which means?" Arthur asked.

"The paint's probably to disguise the trucks, make them look commercial. The lead, and in these massive quantities, means they're doing some serious melting. They're lead-lining at least one of those trailers, maybe all of them."

"Couldn't they just be rigging those to haul all the toxic waste out of there?"

"You apparently haven't seen the rigs they have to use to haul nuclear waste, Wally." Dennis looked thoughtful. Arthur owed himself a kick for ever thinking him a dim bulb. "Nuclear waste has to be solid to be moved doesn't it, Huff?"

Huff nodded, fought back a smile.

"And I've seen the trucks they use to move it. The tractors have a sleeper and the flat bed carries a couple of canisters, looks like a giant dumbbell, at least the ones I've seen. The route any of these takes has to be approved in advance and has to go around major metropolitan areas. Whatever they're doing with these tractor-trailer rigs here isn't the orthodox usual approved method."

"Right." Huff got all the way to a grin. "In the past thirty years there have been an average of around a hundred transports a year and the feds and locals have been informed on every one of them. Something different is definitely going on here. Even if this was a trip to an authorized waste dump, all the nearest dump sites are pretty used up. The people of Ohio wisely resisted letting another dump site open, and the government is trying hard to open new sites elsewhere. It spent seven billion of our tax dollars preparing the Yucca Mountain area north of Las Vegas figuring it could take the land back from the Native Americans there in the way it has operated for centuries. But the Western Shoshone tribe said, 'Nothing doing,' even given the massive bribe they were offered. The government shifted its attention to West Texas, but the people there gave them the one-fingered salute too."

"All true," Arthur said, "but you're straying a little off course."

"The point is, these are the wrong kind of trucks to take uranium anywhere very far. So it's probably a shuttle of the stuff to somewhere in this state, maybe in this county, in a disguised truck. I've run the color types they're using to paint the rigs against any of the major commercial truck lines, either corporate or hauling. The combination coming back points toward one company logo: Sysco Foods."

"They're sure enough going to try to move the stuff, aren't they? But why four trucks?" Rod asked. It seemed a pretty good question.

"That's where things get tricky." Huff looked to Arthur. "If you were sketching this based on what you know, what kind of story line would we have here?"

"We know that Steve has hedged his bet in every enterprise he's ever been involved in, right?"

Huff nodded, but Wally said, "What's that mean?"

"It means," Huff said, "that he always has a backup plan. It's like you're betting on a horse to win at the races, but you bet on another horse to place or show so if you lose your main bet your loses aren't as great as they might have been, or in some cases you don't lose at all. Arthur's right. I've kept an eye on Steve and he's always hedged."

"All I can say is you have way too much time on your hands, Huff," Dennis said.

The others agreed but did not need to say so.

Arthur made eye contact with each of them. "The trucks mean he plans to move the two warheads worth of weapons-grade uranium to another place. He must feel that the risk of a leak to the likes of us, or worse, the feds, is bigger than the risk of moving the stuff. The size and shape of the cabs tells me it isn't far. Why four trucks? To go four directions. Three will be decoys. Now, here's the juicy part. If I wrote this, I'd make the fed in charge, Gerald Benton, an ambitious S.O.B. who knows about the hedge uranium. But he's federal, through and through, and wants the plant's new centrifuge system to succeed. What he wouldn't mind is an international coup—one he can catch in the act, that is. He could grab some high profile headlines and take away Steve's hedge all in one swoop. Then Steve would have to buckle down and make his centrifuge system work, or else."

"You think Benton knows about us but is giving us just enough slack to play things so they benefit him?" Huff said.

"Yeah, that's the part that bothers me," Arthur admitted. "I suspect he doesn't like us for the stars when all the dust settles and the flashbulbs are going off. But I don't know just who he has in mind for it."

Arthur paused, looked around. He could have really used a sip of water. That was asking a lot of a storage shed.

"What Benton really needs is an international group behind the pressure on Steve to move the stuff. If events were orchestrated just right, Steve would get nervous and do just what he's doing. He takes the stuff out of the plant area before any sudden inspection and hides it. Moving it is the opportunity for the foreign power—let's say North Korea or Iran, for verisimilitude—to hit the truck and take the uranium to do something with it, a bomb, a threat, or worse, to blackmail an nation."

"I've got an idea that might round out your picture," Dennis said. "What do you make of this? When he got here, the first thing Benton asked Bob Kennedy is if anyone in the department spoke Spanish."

"Spanish?"

"Yeah, so I got thinking. A week or two back we had a gun violation. Clerk at a gas station says he got a peek at a gun tucked in the belt of a guy pumping gas and makes a call. We pull the guy over, me and a backup car and find the gun. Guess what kind?"

Dennis did not give any of them a chance to guess. "A Liberator. You don't see those often. In fact, I'd never seen one before. But I've heard of them. Frankie probably has too. They're a cheap mass-produced assassination automatic stamped out of steel. The CIA dropped thousands of them all over South America back in the 1940s to help guerilla bands. It was the kind of pal we as a country were to Latin America back in the day. Anyway, they're cheap pieces of crap. The butt only carries loose shells and you have to pop the spent casing out of the barrel with a pencil or a stick. They're just a glorified zip gun, but to some they're a status symbol and blast from the past, like wearing a Che Guevara t-shirt, only a pistol that still shoots is a stronger symbol."

"What about it?" Wally asked. "Doesn't sound like much of a threat if it's just a piece of shit gun."

"We got a Glock nine off him too," Dennis said. "The Lib was just sort of a good luck piece from the guy's past, his father, I'd guess. Turned out to be bad luck this time."

Frankie looked away, either impatient or thinking of something else.

"The kicker is who bailed the guy out, this Ernesto something or other. It was Astrid Lazo. Does that name ring a bell?"

"Isn't she the woman Steve Hamilton was last hooked up with?" Arthur asked.

"Exactly. From Venezuela. And Ernesto, by the way, skipped on his bail and hasn't been seen since. But I do know that Astrid was staying at an RV court, which makes sense for her. That way she's not registered at some motel, though I doubt she'd use her real name. We were lucky to get a peek at her passport for Ernesto's bail."

"So you think it's a crew from Venezuela after the uranium. That clicks. They have lots of reasons not to like the U.S., and I heard Astrid was active. It's one reason Steve backed away from her." Huff panned the faces of the others, ended fixed on Frankie.

"That's pretty wild stuff," Wally said.

"Yeah, but while you were talking, chills ran up and down my spine like a couple of rabid mice," Rod said.

"Bottom line: it's believable."

"It's credible, all right," Dennis agreed. "The questions are: how did this come about, and what are we to do about it? It sounds to me exactly the way it will go down."

"I don't know," Huff said. "It might have one or two more wrinkles to iron out. What do you say, Frankie?"

Frankie's mouth tightened into a thin line.

"What are you saying about Frankie?" Dennis asked.

"The thing is," Huff said, "if this plays the way Arthur just described, then Mr. Gerald "Your Tax Dollars At Work" Benton is willing to sustain some minor collateral damage for the greater good, and what is more expendable than a bunch of half-baked rubes from Ohio."

"Poppy—is expendable?" Rod said, "and Paul was?" His hands began to curl again into massive fists, but he didn't know what to be mad at for sure.

"You think the feds wouldn't let one or two lives in small town America fall under the wheel for what they view as the greater good?" Huff said. "And we're talking here about one who might've slipped off onto his own agenda."

"Let me ask again." Dennis ran a finger along his chin. "What are you saying about Frankie?"

"I'm not going to go out of my way to say anything unsubstantiated or negative," Huff said. "But there is one harsh fact to consider. None of this started until Frankie came back to this area."

"And Poppy?"

"She wouldn't be missing, perhaps dead by now."

*   *   *

Everth Picón Cato sat at the RV's breakfast nook table and missed no detail of Astrid pouring the warmed *leche* and *café* simultaneously into his mug, the soft brown skin of her arms flashing a hint of muscle. He wished he had the moment with her to himself without the nervous chatter of Rodrigo and Victor. He could wish for many things, but the first thing he would want would be to have her as *esposa* instead of *jefe*. But it did no good to think of that just now.

She brought the plates of *frijoles negro y arroz con plátanos verde*. It was a meal on which to go to war. They had all been working toward this day, and here it was at last. He should feel the unrest, the butterflies the others felt, but instead stayed fixed on Astrid. She sat down with them and they ate and drank their *café*. He savored the grit of coffee grounds that had not been filtered out against his teeth.

Her face appeared calm, but he knew the mask. The fire that burned in his belly had been from the first moment to follow the will of *el presidente* and treat the *Americanos* as they deserved. But something far deeper drove Astrid, whose smooth skin matched the *café con leche* and hid those muscles that came from much training. He knew what it was. He had seen her train the way they all did, drive herself when there was no need for the daughter of rich parents. She could have lived a life in the finest hotels instead of out here with them. But no.

He had a different fire in his belly now, but it meant

nothing to her. He knew that. Her focus was rigid and aimed elsewhere. He had seen the smoldering embers in her eyes and knew the passion could never be for him. Perhaps it was as well. She would be more than most men could handle now—best she take it out on someone else, this man who wronged her long ago. Maybe when it was over she could see Everth Picón Cato for the first time, maybe not. He would see. She took an angry bite and chewed as she looked away, as if tasting ashes, or nothing. Who knew? What other *jefe* would cook and serve a meal? There was hope. Perhaps there could be love . . . or death in a rain of bullets. Either way, it was living. These *Americanos* know nothing of passion, to breathe each breath as if it were a last one. To die well, if need be, or to live hard, and fully. He sipped the coffee. Strong. *Bueno.* To taste as much as one can taste, to feel all that can be felt. He watched the smooth brown curve of her cheek as she chewed. Today would be a great day, a savage of a day, no matter what.

Chapter Eighteen

There were a number of ways Frankie could respond, and perhaps he chose the wisest of them. "Arthur, you're the only one who ever consistently beat Steve at chess in high school. You know the patterns of his mind better than anyone."

"That was forty years ago, Frank." Arthur resisted the urge to lift a hand and sweep it through his salt and pepper hair.

"How did he play the game? What was his usual approach?"

"I don't know how this is going to help, but he almost always opened with a Ruy Lopez and sooner or later got around to a queen's gambit declined."

"That, in a nutshell, is what we have to count on here. A gambit using the queen he has," Frankie held up a finger. "Chances are, the truck that rolls out with the uranium in it will have Poppy on board."

"Where do you get that?" Rod rumbled. If he had a beef about Frankie seizing the leadership role again he kept it to himself this time.

"The possibility of exposure at the plant is going to make him want to get rid of or hide two things. One is the set-aside uranium. The other is Poppy. We just need to find

161

out *when* the trucks are going to pull out. Dennis, can you get yourself assigned to something near the plant?"

"There are overtime deputy details that watch the plant day and night. Blame that on Bob Kennedy sucking up to the FBI. Let me come back to this when I've heard what you have to say."

"Why can't we let the police, deputies, or the feds handle the whole thing from this point on?" Rod wanted to know.

"Because Steve will react, and the reaction won't be good for Poppy," Arthur said. "Right now he thinks he can get his hands on Frankie with her, maybe me too. He was counting on some sort of code of honor, no doubt. Besides he may even have a way to hear exactly what we're up to."

Each of them looked around at each other, but most eyes ended up fixed on Frankie, whose face flushed pink and his hands twitched, starting to curl into fists. It was the first time that Arthur felt genuinely threatened by him. He thought Frankie might swing first and explain later. A perverse side of him enjoyed Frankie's discomfort, enjoyed it a lot.

"Easy," Rod cautioned. "You bailed us out back there, but that don't make you no leader of the pack. I'd like to hear what Arthur and Huff have to say. They got some pretty fine brains on themselves, they do."

Frankie's face grew pink all the way to his temples. He looked ready to explode. His hands curled tight, then eased open again. He took a deep breath. "It's stuffy in here. I'm going to take a short hike and be back."

The sound of his steps on the gravel retreated. Wally waited until they had faded out of hearing before he spoke. "Whew. I thought he was going to let us all have it there for a minute. I don't mind telling you I was ready to fall over in a faint if he so much as jumped in my direction. Who would have ever thought he would be one of the bad asses to come out of our class?"

"I don't know. I could take him," Rod said, squaring his shoulders and sucking in his gut.

"Yeah, but you have the heart of a teddy bear," Wally said. "Now Rolly, he might be more than a match."

"Rolly's a bully, that's true. But you forget about Donnie Angel. I was at elementary with Donnie Angel when he graduated from pulling the wings off flies to setting pet hamsters on fire." Dennis suppressed a shudder. "Now there is someone I hope I never have to try and arrest."

"Isn't he living with . . .?"

"Yeah, Wally. He's shacking up with Mary Ann Reznick these days. Now there's something to picture. I'd imagine the castle has gone quite Goth these days." Dennis grinned. "To tell the truth, I don't even like to drive by the place in the cruiser."

Arthur did not let himself think of Donnie Angel when he could help it, but had only a day or two ago, seemed like a lifetime now, been thinking how he usually skipped briskly past Donnie's face when he looked through the old class yearbook. It made him shiver. He realized he had been repressing even thinking about Donnie. Rolly might beat people cross-eyed, but Donnie Angel made Arthur's skin crawl. In school, Donnie had not avoided Rolly. He did not avoid anyone. It was the other way around, because you just never knew which direction Donnie would leap. He could have been a top athlete, but chose not to participate in sports. He was tall, six-seven or so, and rawhide tough. He liked getting into fights more than competing for the school.

In their senior year Donnie starred as the central player in an incident. At the drive-in movie, Ben Kendorf, a two-hundred pound tuba player spotted Donnie's girl, tiny Suzie Mackentyre, sitting alone in Donnie's car. He said something flirting and playful to her and turned to see Donnie coming toward them with popcorn and a couple of sodas on a cardboard tray. Donnie dropped the tray. Popcorn and soda spilled everywhere, and he kept coming. Ben never really recalled what exactly he had said to Suzie, except he thought it was harmless enough. Years later, under hypnosis in a therapy session in Florida to deal with bad dreams, Suzie came up with the line. "Hey, Suzie. The cat's away. What say you and me play?"

Donnie's big fists and long arms were going when he reached Ben, who held up the flats of his hands in hopes of ironing out any confusion. In front of a small crowd of witnesses who said they were helpless to interfere, Donnie beat Ben into a shattered lump. Ben later said he had slipped and hit his head on a bumper. He never once threw a punch. His friends later wanted to gang up on Donnie, but Ben asked them not to, this in spite of Donnie having dragged the limp Ben to the car to slam his right hand in the car door again and again while some watchers screamed, moaned, and even threw up. Ben not only never played the tuba again he couldn't even pick up a pencil with that hand. On the slim bright side, it kept him out of Viet Nam. He became an accountant and in time moved to Seattle where he became part of the stats that proclaimed the all too frequent gray-sky area "the suicide capital of America." Several of those who had watched and been afraid to interfere that night at the drive-in said Donnie had smiled the whole time like a kid at Christmas.

He was just about the most intense individual Arthur had ever known. He had tried to use him in fiction a time or two but Donnie Angel was far beyond villain. Arthur could not imagine Mary Ann living with him, although she was said to be a handful and maybe after being with Steve it took someone like Donnie to be interesting to her.

Arthur stared off between the rows of storage units toward a sky that did not seem certain about what it wanted to do next, tangle into a knot of rain clouds or burst apart in a sunlit wash of blue. From the center of his chest he felt a sudden warm rush spread out as a lot of loose pieces came together to form a picture, an understanding that felt so clear and immediate it caused him to miss a breath or two. He thought at first the emotion he felt was fear, but it wasn't. It was awareness, and resolution, so firm none of it needed to be thought about or a decision made. It would happen. It was what had to happen, what he had to make happen.

Wally and Rod stood close to Dennis, engrossed in a more recent story he shared about the dark side of Donnie

Angel that had evolved into a discussion of who would come out on top if Donnie and Rolly Stanton ever went at it face to face.

Arthur looked up along the row of storage doors. Frankie was quite a ways from them. Good.

Huff saw whatever had swept across Arthur's face and leaned closer so Arthur could say in a low voice, "Maybe Poppy had the best take on things all along, this mess, hell, on life. It hasn't done her a lot of good, but she was right. Give her that, though I might never get the chance to admit that to her. You can't live a whole and fulfilling life off alone in some hole hiding from people all your life, no matter how cushy you've made the nest. You have to get out there and get the dirt of involvement with humanity all the way under your fingernails, to earn the right to coexist in grace and in anything close to dignity."

"Do you mean me?" Huff said.

"I mean all of us."

"You know, you're not being as clear as you may think," Huff said.

"That's okay. I'll get more so. I can envision how the insides of this whole thing might unfold like some ugly and crippled flower. It's all tighter than I thought, though far from tidy, or easy. The main thing right now, at least for me, is Poppy."

"What do you have in mind?" Huff said in a near whisper.

Louder, Arthur said. "Man, when was the last time we ate? That may be what has some of us edgy."

"Yeah," Rod said. "I could eat the butt off a skunk."

"One of us who isn't public enema number one might dash and get some burgers," Huff said. He looked at Arthur.

Arthur dug in his bag and came out with a hundred dollar bill. He handed it to Wally. "That ought to do it."

"I'll go with," Rod said. "You drive, Wally."

As soon as the green truck pulled away, Huff said, "What have you got, Arthur?"

Dennis moved closer, one eyebrow lifting into an arch.

"We don't have much time. I'll go through this quickly," Arthur said. He reached for a clipboard that hung off Huff's pegboard. A pencil was attached by a string. He started writing quickly. "We're going to need a few things."

Dennis' forehead wrinkled and he edged closer. He looked at Huff, then glanced down the row of storage sheds. Frankie walked along the far chain link fence, talking into a cell phone. "What's going on here?"

"I'll tell you the whole thing." Arthur handed the clipboard to Huff. "Can you pick up all this stuff without making a splash?"

"Hell, I've got some of it here. Most of the surveillance sound equipment stuff. Tell us where you're going with this."

Arthur did. Dennis and Huff leaned in close and hung on every word. When he was done he glanced at his watch and saw the story took only seven and a half minutes to lay out for them. He took a couple of bundles of money from his bag and gave it to Huff. "This should do for our expenses. Judging from your home security, Huff, I'm guessing you were a good customer at that police supply and security equipment warehouse out on Broad. Were you a good enough customer to get them to open at this hour for you?"

Huff nodded, and added a wink. "It's bloody brilliant. That's what it is."

"Huff, when we get done with this, *if* we get done with this, no more BBC for a while. Okay?" Arthur kept an eye on his watch and listened for steps on the gravel.

"Holy crap?" Dennis scratched an eyebrow. "You really want to do this? It's risky."

"I'm staking Poppy's life on it."

"And your own."

"There's that. It's the only way we can be certain to get Poppy back. Before this is over, we may even have to make Frankie a hero."

"Are you kidding? What about the others? Could they let us down?"

"I'm counting on it, Dennis. Expecting it, at least." Arthur stopped. The steps on gravel coming their way grew louder until Frankie appeared at the storage shed door.

"What're you three blind mice going on about?"

"Arthur has a plan, and it's sterling plated," Dennis said.

"Go ahead. I could use a laugh."

"We can go over it while we eat. Here are the guys with our burgers." Arthur nodded toward the truck. Rod stepped out of the passenger side with a sack he could barely handle.

"Holy cow. Do you think he spent the whole hundred on burgers?" Huff said.

"Wouldn't be surprised."

Rod had only spent half the hundred, but that was still a lot of bacon cheeseburgers, with onion rings and fries. They all squatted on the floor and passed around napkins, packets of mustard, and sipped from their sodas. Arthur could not remember when last he had eaten a meal. It could be a while before he ate another one. This was no time to think about a diet. Once the mood had grown calmer and Arthur felt as stuffed as a human can get, he pushed away a pile of wrappers and shared only the part he intended with the others.

"The way I picture it, there will be four trucks coming out of the plant in the four basic directions. Only one of them will contain the uranium, but I figure that one will also have Poppy in it. Dennis will try to find out the time."

"I think I can help you with that. I could have said something earlier, but wanted to hear more first." The corner of Dennis' mouth twisted into a wry smile. "Bob Kennedy and a handful of his select deputies will be working the plant surveillance tonight. It's the first time for that, and I figure there's a reason."

"You're right. The trucks will probably make their run tonight. Well, that solves another wrinkle for us, but puts us under a deadline. Looks like we need the rest of the stuff now, Huff. Wally and Rod have homes, but Frankie, Huff and I were probably going to have to sleep in the storage shed or somewhere worse."

"It's Frank. Can you just lay off the Frankie business for a while?"

"Okay, Frankie," Arthur said. "So, it's tonight. That doesn't leave us much time to prepare. If we're lucky, we'll be able to determine which truck has Poppy. If not, we'll need to follow all four. We've got Dennis' truck and Wally's truck, and Rod has a bike."

"That leaves us a vehicle short." Dennis looked to Arthur.

"I used to have one. It went up with the house."

Huff was suppressing a grin. "I might have an idea." He rose and waved to the others. They got up in varying degrees of speed after having eaten too much. Rod pushed the rest of a burger into his mouth and chewed as he followed. Arthur was pretty sure Rod had eaten at least half a dozen of the burgers and more than his share of the fries and rings as well. Well, he was stoking a big furnace.

At the door to the storage shed next to his, Huff fiddled at the lock and swung the door open. He stepped in and flipped on the light.

"Oh, my god." Dennis was the first to speak. "A Lotus Cortina."

The squat squarish retro-looking two-door car was white with green stripes that flared back into near fins with tail lights that looked like the Mercedes symbol. Arthur thought it looked like something out of the very oldest James Bond movies, something a young Sean Connery would have driven.

"Yeah" Huff sighed. "A 1967 Mk. II dual overhead

cam model, the one made on the Dagenham production line. Some people bad mouth it, say it doesn't have the power and handling of the Mk. I. But think of the year. It's the car I wanted when I graduated and I was twenty years getting my hands on one, and this one is near mint."

"It's a shame to take it out on the road," Arthur admitted, "but we need it."

"Not a very inconspicuous car, is it," Frankie said.

"How could you dare drive it?" Wally said. "What if something happens to it?"

"I can't see we have much choice, unless one of you wants to call Avis."

"We'll need communication too," Wally said.

Huff stepped away and came back from the other storage shed with four Trac cell phones. "Each has a hundred hours paid in advance, and these shouldn't be traceable. But use them only when you have to. The other phones are set up on the speed dials."

"You've been living for this moment, haven't you?" Frankie said.

Arthur noticed that Frankie's spirits had seemed to lift in the last few moments. He no longer looked ready to tear each of them a new asshole.

"I need to borrow your truck, Wally and pick up a few things. Okay?" Huff held out a hand and Wally handed him the keys. He was watching Rod make a phone call.

"No, I won't be home for a while, Bitsy. All right? Yeah, Wally's still here and he's okay. Why?" Rod paced slowly up the row of sheds and they heard no more of the conversation.

Arthur watched a smile ease into place on Wally's formerly troubled face. The wayward eye seemed to skitter off to look at the stars, which were just beginning to come out.

The lights from the open storage shed doors cast a yellow glow on the others. Huff pulled out in Wally's truck and headed toward town.

"Where's he going?" Frankie asked.

"Oh, just to get a few things we might need on a contingency basis."

"Still don't trust me, Arthur?"

"Don't tell me some of Huff's conspiracy theory neurosis has rubbed off on you?"

Rod took the sidecar off his bike, parked that in the shed, and rumbled off to stay near the plant and let them know if anything started to happen. He had shoved a couple of the leftover burgers into one saddlebag, just in case.

"Man must have a tapeworm," Frankie said. His spirits sure seemed improved.

While Huff was gone they used his laptop to see what they could learn about the hunt for Arthur. Frankie's name had still not been mentioned. Arthur was still a prize to anyone who could lay hands on him.

Arthur glanced to Dennis and only saw a line or two of worry wrinkle his brow.

Dennis climbed into his truck to take a nap, saying he would need to be alert later.

Arthur and Frankie traded restless glances in the storage shed, wondering who would push for first shift for a nap on the back seat of a forty-year-old car. Arthur finally waved a hand. "You first." Being around people so long had put him on edge. He doubted if he could sleep anyway, especially after learning about himself on the national news services.

It was nearly midnight when Huff got back with Wally's truck. It had gotten as dark outside as it could get.

Frankie climbed out of the back seat. Huff was loading boxes into the trunk of the Lotus Cortina.

"What did you need that took you over two and a half hours to locate?" Frankie asked.

Huff took a couple of pistols out of one box and handed them to Frankie. "These are for Arthur and Wally. I got revolvers for them. Easier to use. Show them how to load and use them."

"Ah, a little black market shopping." Frankie smiled.

Arthur took one of the revolvers, a Smith and Wesson .38 with an inch long barrel. It would be just dandy if someone was willing to walk almost into the end of it. "I know a bit about guns, Frankie."

"Let him at least show Wally a thing or two," Huff said. He kept loading more boxes into the trunk.

Frankie led Wally off to the other storage shed, probably to bore him with basics he already knew. Dennis climbed out of the truck and went along to watch, at least without laughing out loud.

When it was just the two of them, Huff bent close to Arthur and said, "Are you afraid?"

"Hell, yes." Arthur could feel his insides trembling away like a dozen small earthquakes trying to work up to a gallop.

"How are you—what are you going to do about it?"

"Not much I can do. Just stay busy and focused on Poppy. She's what matters right now."

"I just wish all this would happen faster," Huff said, "or not at all. My guts are doing the left-handed Mexican jumping bean dance."

Arthur's phone rang. "Careful what you wish for, Huff," he said, though he felt glad for the interruption. It was Rod.

"Better saddle up all of you," Rod said. "It's about to get busy over here."

Chapter Nineteen

Gerald Benton watched his men pull on their tactical gear. He warmed inside with the pride of ownership that comes from heading a squad of some of the best trained, best equipped, and most capable men ever assembled. They checked their belts, pouches, and weapons for the second or third time, tightening straps and testing communications. They loaded the three black vans with the spotlights, speakers, and the rest of the gear. In spite of only a small butterfly or two he felt good, damned good.

For all they knew, everyone was in the loop and they were all following orders. He had known all along that as soon as he sent something as big as this up the pipeline it would be taken from him, be someone else's feather. There was some risk here, but he was damn well not going to let that happen. This was going to be *his* headline. He would be as big as Patton or MacArthur in their best days.

He rehearsed a couple of sound bites in his head and pictured headlines, both newspaper and follow-up magazine spreads. This was the mother lode. The story was all the sweeter for that ass of a president of Venezuela, who had publicly gone after the U.S. for interfering, because of oil. The man even called the former U.S. president "the devil." Well, the damn fool was just lucky we hadn't gone in there and blown him out of the water the way America was wont to do when dealing with other countries that resisted the wide-spread need for petroleum.

Benton had even taken to keeping an eye on Air Force One, cautioning each time it was used, "Now don't you wreck my plane." It was only a matter of time, and after tonight the momentum was going to pick up in earnest.

He caught his reflection in one of the vans' tinted windows and squared his shoulders. One arm was almost an inch longer than the other and Rodriguez, who had gone through Quantico with him, had busted his chops about the drape of his suits until Benton had taken every suit and jacket to the tailor Rodriguez suggested on Cincinnati's Delta Avenue. "Keep your good side to the camera and tuck your chin down a bit so it doesn't look like the bow of a destroyer," he had advised. He should know. His media air time these days was in D.C. Damned Bureau ethnic diversity program had shot him up through the ranks like a greased bar of soap. *We'll see who's getting the high profile air time now.* He had spent a half hour on the knot of his tie and he had shaved close enough for the aftershave to burn. He turned the other way. Rodriguez was right. He did have a good side.

Well, they should all be ready, including that uptight twit from the local NBC affiliate who kept bugging him to let him ride along the next time something interesting was about to happen. Their mouths will be hanging open this time.

He stepped out where as many of the men as possible could see him and called out, "Okay, men. Let's go do this."

Chapter Twenty

"Nervous?" Arthur asked.

"Hell, yes. Aren't you?" Wally rubbed the back of his hand across his lips and stared straight ahead to where his headlights cut uneven swaths of road. His truck seemed to have one slightly wandering eye as well. He bent forward and gripped the wheel tightly, as if its surface felt oily.

"Don't you think we're playing with fire?" Wally's wayward eye seemed to shoot in rapid clicks to several directions.

"I wish there was another choice. Sit at home and hope this all comes out all right and that Poppy is swept up by the FBI and protected? If I could see it that way, and if I had a home to sit in, I'd sure be there."

"So Rod spots which truck she's in and we all converge before the FBI stops the truck, and we rescue Poppy, somehow without getting shot at."

"Oh, we might get shot at."

"There are too many things that could go wrong. What's the FBI supposed to be doing this whole time?"

"They don't want to move too soon. They have to wait until Astid Lazo and her Venezuelans have the uranium, then the Bu team sweeps in and Benton is the hero of the moment and all attention is away from Steve and on a foreign power. They want Steve to succeed, no matter what. Benton also very much wants to capture a foreign team with nuclear interests. That would be a huge feather in his hat. My only objective is to keep any harm from coming to Poppy."

"I'm more worried about harm coming to us." Wally's voice had picked up a touch of quiver. He stared ahead at the road as if all the answers lay there.

Arthur guided his turns and told him when to pull over. "Now we wait," he said.

Wally parked his small green pickup truck so it crowded up to thick growth poking through a three-strand barbed-wire fence on Arthur's side. It did not help the claustrophobia he felt both of being close to another person and crowded inside the small truck's cab.

"Why did you pick the West direction for us?"

"I had a hunch about that route."

"You're sure about how they're going to do this?"

"There might be some exceptions. Let's give it a rest for now, Wally."

"Just for the record . . ."

"Yes, Wally?"

". . . I think your plan sucks."

Arthur looked at Wally, who stared out his side window now, a nervous twitch showing when one ear jerked.

"Frankie seemed to like it. He went along."

"You haven't figured out Frankie yet? You're an idiot, Arthur."

"I guess we all have a side to play. What's going on

with you and Bitsy?"

"Nothing. That wasn't who I called back at the storage sheds either."

"I doubt it was, Wally. There was no need if Rod had already told her you were okay. I imagine that made her feel better."

"Yeah, there's Rod. You think I'm some sort of pond scum, don't you?"

"Hey, I'm in no position to judge anyone, Wally. I'm having a little trouble sorting out what's right and wrong myself just now. But if you bring a little passion and tenderness into anyone's life, well, my hat's off to you. You're doing more good than I ever have."

"You haven't been exactly a player, have you?" Wally muttered.

"You're right there," Arthur admitted. "I've always been a brickhead about romance, a late bloomer at the very least. Did you know I graduated from high school a virgin?"

"Why are you telling me this?"

"To pass the time. I was a scribbler even back then, kept to myself and never dated once."

"That was because of your thing for Poppy. Everyone knew about it, pitiful and sad as it was."

"There's that. But I want to tell you about the time I showed up at school with beer. You see, one afternoon three fellows I thought were pretty cool asked me to go out on a ride with them. I didn't hesitate. I leaped. This was the camaraderie I was missing. So they got me to buy some beer, even though I was under age, which I figured was part of the initiation. We rode around and ended up out by the Higgins farm."

"That was a parking spot."

"I know, but kids drank there too as well as made out. Besides, it was early and I had to get to play practice soon. I had a bit part while Poppy was one of the stars. We sat out there and each drank a beer and talked. After a while they looked at each other and drove me back to school and dropped me off with what was left of the six pack. I was stashing it my locker when Poppy caught me. She was ticked because I was late and the practice was running long because of it. I took the beer out to a dumpster instead but still got stung for bringing the beer into the school, even on hearsay evidence. That's the way it was back then."

"I don't know why you're telling me this now, of all times."

Arthur reached up and touched the tender spot in the thick of his hair behind his ear where Huff has slipped the tiny GPS tracker chip in under his scalp and sutured it into place. The spot was still sore, but the slight scab had hardened. He resisted the urge to pick at it. "You see, I played back everything those guys said in the car and it wasn't until a few years after the incident that I figured out they were trying to see, since I didn't date girls, if I was gay. I wasn't. I was just socially out of step, which is why it took me so long to even figure out their agenda."

"Who were they?"

"Oh, that doesn't matter now. Neither Rod nor Paul, if that's what you were thinking. Most of them married, I believe, and went on to live regular lives. That was just an experimental phase, something I was unaware about at the time. Who knows if they step out and walk on the wild side now and then on their wives? We all have a few dark secrets and I know very few people who have been completely faithful through the span of years."

"You're talking about me again, aren't you?"

"No. I'm just pondering the imponderables."

"Such as?"

"Wally, you ever have a moment where everything you knew, believed, lived all your life seemed wrong, and empty?"

"Everyone has that, now and then."

"I don't mean an occasion twitch, or pang. I mean when you completely flip-flop, head a whole new direction, toward meaning, and can't go back to the way you'd been going."

"Still sounds like you're talking about my life?"

"I'm talking about anything strong enough, desirable enough for you to risk everything."

"Yeah, I've been there, done that, got the t-shirt."

"You can make light of it, but it's hard to deal with, harder than anything I've gone through in the past couple of days. It means admitting I know a lot less than I thought I did, about anyone or anything. It also means digging at myself and admitting where I've been stingy when I thought I was giving, where I've kept myself apart from what I should have embraced, and where I didn't even let myself care, need, or admit what I really want. Ever been there?"

"I think you know I have, if you're hinting at what I think you are."

"I'm not hinting. I'm talking about universal truths everyone experiences more often than they know. The awareness is what is most often missing."

"Okay. Okay. I made that leap. Trust me. It doesn't matter what anyone thinks, either. Look at me. You've heard the guys busting my chops about working in a convenience store. I'm worse off than that. I'm heading toward retirement age with nothing to count on, damn little Social Security and no pension. I'm gonna be one of those gray-haired toothless guys you see greeting everyone at a Wal-Mart store. Big deal. I know where my life's headed and there's damn all little I can do about it. But I do have one thing, though it's not even mine, and no one can take that away from me. Don't think the mess I'm in didn't take courage and sacrifice to get here. Can you understand?"

"I might not have a few days ago, but I do now."

Any response Wally intended to make stopped when both their phones rang at once. Rod had hit the conference call speed dial.

"We've got a problem, guys," he said. "The trucks came out of the plant and there's a girl in each cab."

"Damn," Wally muttered.

They both hung up. "Looks like we all get to play." Arthur waited for Wally to open the door on his side so they could both get out.

"Don't sound so damned happy about it," Wally muttered. He got out and Arthur followed. They each picked up a couple of the Phoenix magnum spike strips. These were around twenty pounds apiece and Huff had said they would do the trick on a semi, stopping it within a mile. They had better. They had been far from cheap.

"I would have far preferred the group of us having a go at the truck. The driver is almost certainly armed." Wally got into position on the far side of the road. Arthur stayed to the near side. Some sort of bird made an irritating repetitive sound in the woods behind him that began to pluck at Arthur's already strained nerves.

"Lights coming," Wally sang out.

Arthur could see them fine. He got ready. First, make sure it's a semi. He held one strip ready to slap into place, the other hanging over his back with the spike side out so he could sling it into place next. Between them they could cover the whole two lane country road.

The lights dipped down a hill and started up until brighter and brighter. The beams popped over the rise and Arthur leaped forward.

"Wait," Wally called out.

Arthur stopped, eased back until he was as far off the road as he could get and half concealed by leaves he hoped were not poison ivy.

The truck whooshed past, a white pickup hauling a single horse trailer.

He let his breath out slowly and eased back up to the side of the road to wait. The semi should be next.

They waited. Arthur glanced to the luminous dial of his watch. Ten minutes went by. The wind tugged at the leaves in the woods and critters moved in restless night prowling along the forest floor. The stars grew brighter and the shadows darker. "Something's not right," he finally said.

They both tossed their strips into the back of the truck and Wally jockeyed the Ranger around until they headed the other direction.

A mile down the road from where they had waited a Sysco semi was pulled over beside the road.

Wally eased to the side of the road, and while the truck was still moving Arthur swung the door open and pulled the hammer back on the revolver he held. He ran across the road, fixed on the woman's shape in the front seat. The driver's side was empty. He stepped up on the passenger side and swung the door open. "The woman's an inflatable doll," he yelled.

"Yeah, and the back doors are open and there are a couple of ramps back here."

"The horse trailer," Arthur mumbled.

He stepped down from the truck and started around the front of the truck. "We need to . . ."

"I don't think so." That was sure not Wally's voice.

Arthur turned around slowly just as the flashlight beam switched on and blinded him. He could barely make out the person holding the light except to note that the head was higher up than his own.

"Just take it easy and everything will be okay, Arthur. Donnie won't hurt you." Now that was Wally's voice. He stood beside Donnie Angel.

Boy, this stinks. Arthur didn't get time for more than the one brief thought before a foot swung up and slammed into his stomach as hard as he'd ever been kicked. The gun fell from his hand and he jack-knifed and tumbled sideways to the ground, throwing up as he fell.

From where he lay in the vomit-covered grass he heard the sounds of a struggle.

"Wait. Wait. You said . . ."

He could make them out in the light of the flashlight Donnie had dropped to the ground. Donnie held Wally from behind and was bending him. Arthur wanted to just lie there. He felt broken inside. But he forced himself to push at the ground until he was upright. His legs wobbled, yet he ran toward them and heard a sharp crack just before he got there. Donnie let go of Wally's body. It slumped to the ground, a look of terror on Wally's face and the one wayward eye really staring off at nothing this time.

Donnie swept a backhand hard across Arthur's face that snapped his head hard to the left. "I sure get a kick out of you," Donnie said as a foot landed in Arthur's ribs. He felt a sharp pain and was falling again.

Donnie picked up the flashlight and walked over toward him. He caught a glimpse of Wally's body and then Donnie's large suede shoes blocked the view. The shoes looked soft, but they sure hadn't felt that way.

"Hey, steel-toed hush puppies. Get it? I figured you writer types would enjoy a good oxymoron better than the next guy."

Donnie bent forward and his face loomed close. His intense eyes never blinked. His grin was wide and his teeth very white against his dark tan. The face eased back away as he straightened upright and Arthur heard him laughing.

185

Then a foot slammed into his ribs, again and again. He looked up and saw the toe of a shoe coming straight for his head.

*   *   *

Arthur stirred to a head throbbing like his worst hangover ever. One side of his bloody and probably broken nose had stopped up from where it pressed against a plastic drop cloth stretch across the rear floorboards of a moving car.

Donnie heard him. "Don't you be moving or bleeding all over the place back there. Mary Ann just had this heap detailed and she won't be happy if you should make a mess."

"Is it about money, Donnie?"

"It's *always* about money. Where've you been all your life? Try living in a castle with bad insulation too. Power bills alone would make your eyes pop."

"And Wally?'

"Yeah, money hunger with him too. Thought he'd take his little sweety Bitsy off somewhere far from here. Well, his worries about that are all over."

"Did you have to kill him?"

"No. That notion just came to me. You know how those things are. A whim. I might get the same notion about you. Can't predict anything. Might be a full moon, or I might get a sudden dislike for you. Or I might just get a restless

186

twitch. That sort of thing."

The matter of fact way Donnie could talk about killing was no act, and his voice began to send prickles up and down Arthur's arms. Something low in his stomach ached, too low to be a broken rib, though it felt like he might have one or two of those as well. The pain kept him alert.

"Is Poppy okay?"

"Shut up. I'm tired of listening to your rattle of words, word man."

"Donnie, just tell me, is she . . ."

It was as far as he got. Whatever Donnie used was hard, like a tire iron, and he hadn't lost any of his quickness through the years. It was smashed hard into Arthur's temple and forehead. A flash of bright yellow, like a small sunburst exploding, then black. Nothing.

Chapter Twenty One

With its headlights off, the black pickup eased into the roadside rest high on a hill and Dennis reached and turned the engine off. "Nice view from here. You get a good splash of moonlight on the road down there. Behind us, if you turn your head, you can look over and see the castle from here. Lots of folks like to come to this spot to take their pictures. This winding road used to be the main road until they built the straight one down there. Probably were more picnics here then. Nowadays kids come here to park and lose their innocence. I don't know, Frankie. I think it was a better world when there were more winding roads where people took their time. What do you think?"

Frankie started to reach for his door handle until he heard the hammer being drawn back on an automatic. Dennis' left hand was across his lap and he held the gun pointed at Frankie.

"So, it's like that, is it?"

"I don't know quite how it is, yet, Frankie. Why don't we enjoy the show and find out? Reach in the glove box and get the two sets of binoculars. I'll take the smaller Nikon set. You can use the wide angle ones. They're great for sporting events."

They did not have to wait long. A semi pulled around a

curve in the road and rumbled down the hill. Just before it got to the bottom two cement mixers backed out of either side of the road, blocking the way. The sound of the truck hitting its loud engine compression jake brakes to slow to a stop chattered explosively against the surrounding hillsides.

A swarm of figures surrounded the truck. Frankie could see automatic weapons pointed at the cab while two of the men went around to the back. He glanced to Dennis, saw the gun still pointed his way.

The back doors swung open and they heard one of them shout, "*Vacío.*"

A small figure dressed in the same camouflage fatigues as the others only with long dark hair, Astrid Lazo herself, headed toward the truck's cab in angry, quick strides.

"That means empty, doesn't it?" Dennis asked. "Oh, here comes the part I like."

Massive lights clicked on and bathed the scene in a white wash. Three matching black vans rolled out of the woods to block the road in both directions. Loudspeakers boomed in English and Spanish. Men in black with white FBI letters prominently displayed swooped in on all sides. One of the high-jackers began to fire at them and was mowed down by three separate bursts of fire. The others, including the woman, dropped their weapons and held their hands high.

"What do you think Benton will say when he finds there were no nukes on the truck?" Dennis said.

"I imagine he'll be checking the other trucks. The ruse wouldn't have sailed past him." Frankie kept his eyes on the cab. The agents who eventually opened the door and took out the driver also held up one of those inflatable dolls, the kind you can buy at adult book shops. He held it in one hand and waved it.

"What the hell? Where's Poppy then?"

"Like you said, Frankie. There are still three other trucks to check."

"I'm betting they don't find her in any of those either."

"You know, you might just be onto something."

They watched in silence while the truck's driver and Venezuelan cell members were loaded into one of the vans and the other two, with Benton inside, had taken off with an angry chirp of tires before Dennis started his truck, kept the lights off, and eased out of the roadside rest onto the country road. He grinned to himself, but Frankie looked far from being happy.

Chapter Twenty Two

At the first flicker of his eyelids Arthur thought he was having a heart attack. His chest hurt like dammit. Well, I've lived an okay life. I could have loved more, been a part of things, but, what the hell. Couldn't we all? Is there anything in the house I wouldn't want found? No porn? That was ages ago. Oh, the house is gone. I guess that takes care of that.

As he lay there, the pain centralized until he could identify that it focused in just a few ribs. He realized his ticker had not blown, but his skeletal system had been in better shape. His head hurt too, now that he took a quick inventory. His eyes fluttered open.

Poppy's icy pale blue eyes were inches from his own. "Oh, you're alive."

She sure smelled good. Lavender, maybe a hint of musk. At least the one open nostril of his smashed nose still worked.

"Is that a question or disappointed statement?"

"I'm glad you're alive, though you're a ripe bloody mess. Choose the wrong dance partner? It's been cold and dank and lonely in here, and any company's good company."

Arthur's eyes flicked past her and took in the stone

walls, thick rusted metal bars. "The dungeon. I guessed that."

"Here. Sit up. You look like a puddle lying there that way."

"Thanks," he mumbled, flinching each time it felt like his ribs scraped against each other. He felt along his torn shirt. No bones were sticking all the way out, though there were more than a couple spots that made him flinch when he touched them.

Poppy tore a loose piece off his shirt and went across the room with it. The cloth was damp when she used it to dap at dried blood on his face.

"You have running water?"

"Let me acquaint you with the accommodations." Her mouth twisted into a wry half smile. "There are two buckets. One contains water. That's it."

"Can we talk?"

She pointed to an upper corner of the stone room. Arthur could make out the camera lens.

"It listens too. The whole place is wired, I'm told."

"That's sweet."

"I think you've been hit on your head pretty hard. That's what I think." She dabbed as she spoke and each touch of the damp cloth on a bruise felt like he was being hit again.

"Why do you say that?" His teeth clenched tight as she rubbed at a scab on his forehead.

"Imagine, someone as brick-headed as you getting fired up to do things that don't come natural, to get involved in the first place and then try to come and rescue me like some wobbly knight and only get yourself into a worse mess than you were in."

"You don't think I have it in me?"

"I didn't expect you to be able to get past . . ."

"Myself? Well, once I got past my fear of commitment, intimacy, and being beaten up, it was easy."

"Oh, my God. Listen to you babble. Your head's broken for sure."

"Look, I wanted to come so I could be able to tell you that I realized what I like about you was what I thought I disliked." He flinched and felt her touch ease in response.

"What on earth are you talking about?" He could tell from her celery crisp tone he hadn't phrased that as well as he would have liked.

"You're not a tattletale; you're a whistle-blower. When you see something wrong in your community you take action to make it right. A lot of people wouldn't do that, wouldn't get involved. You did. That's a rare thing. Some people might call it a busybody streak but I see it now for what it is: an awareness that things can be better, that something needs to be done. I let my own bias cloud my perspective on that. This latest effort was about giving to your community, not all about getting back at Steve."

"It was a little about that, and guilt. We discussed that. Now, be quiet and rest. You've been banged up pretty good, or I should say pretty bad."

"We all have something to feel a little guilty about," he said. "Not everyone takes the path of redemption. It's liable to be a rocky one."

He winced when she rubbed hard at a spot along the side of his neck. "What did you do? Take on an army?"

"An army of one."

"That would be Donnie Angel." The voice came from outside the bars. "He doesn't know his own strength. No, I take that back. He does, but doesn't care." Mary Ann's keys rattled and the door swung open and clanged closed.

"Are you sure you feel safe coming in here with us? Aren't you afraid we'll try to jump you and take your keys away?"

If there is such a thing as an evil giggle, that was what Mary Ann shared with them. "I was kind of hoping you would try."

Arthur saw the thick black biker boots and panned up from there. Black leather pants. Tight. Very tight. Red silk blouse with puffy sleeves. Pale skin, almost parchment white. Pitch black hair. He seemed to remember her as a redhead. She whirled the big ring of keys in one hand and stared at Poppy, inviting her, daring her.

Give her this, she had come to their high school all those years back as an outsider. Her father's clout changed that. In weeks she had been inserted as a cheerleader and an established member of the squad had been given a subtle boot. That did not endear her to the other cheerleaders, Poppy included. It was water off a duck's back to her, and in a few more weeks she had stolen Steve Hamilton away from Poppy as well. No, there was no love being rekindled here.

"I've got to say I was surprised you got involved in this,

Mary Ann. Isn't Steve ancient history for you?"

"Poor Poppy, willing to take table scraps when I dumped him way back when. I heard all about you making a fool of yourself, putting the horns on Pecky. You always had a thing for Steve. Do you still?"

"Oh, I have a thing for him, but it's not a good thing."

Mary Ann stepped closer until they could hear the creak of her leather pants and see that she was almost without wrinkles except around her eyes and those lines didn't look like they came from laughing. She was sure fit and looked like one more member of their class who stayed in better shape than Arthur. His state of physical being had taken a recent downward turn, thanks to Donnie. But he was in better shape than Wally.

"Wally's dead, by the way, Poppy," he said. "Donnie had something on Wally, enough to make him betray us. He used poor Wally and then killed him out there and tossed him away like he was the unwanted runt of a litter."

"Donnie's not a bad boy. He took me to France for our honeymoon. Isn't that where you wanted to go, Poppy? With Steve, wasn't it? Steve told me once, at a time when he felt relaxed and talkative. You know, in bed."

"Donnie's a low thug, Mary Ann. He always has been. He just never ran into anyone able to physically dispute that. I am surprised that he let Steve involve you in something liable to turn into a pretty sticky mess. There must be big money involved too, and I imagine it takes a good deal of that to maintain a castle like this. Otherwise he'd be too much the jealous type." A fresh lump on Arthur's cheekbone throbbed to the beat of his heart.

Mary Ann stepped closer and swung an experimental toe into his ribs. That bent him double and made her smile. "Donnie Angel doesn't like for people to speak bad about him."

She glanced around at their cell, took in the buckets, then fixed on the camera in the room's upper corner.

"You know, this is where he makes me stay when he thinks I've been bad."

"When's that?" Poppy asked. She helped Arthur sit up until his back was against the stone wall again. She dabbed at the corner of his mouth with the wet cloth. Arthur felt around inside his mouth with his tongue, found a tooth that was loose.

"Oh, a lot of the time." She shuddered. "Naked, you know. There are spiders down here, and rats. You have to stay awake all night or they'll try to eat your fingers, or even your eyes."

"Were you really bad, or is Donnie even more nuts than you are?"

Arthur thought Poppy was picking at a scab he would have left alone.

Mary Ann's eyes glittered and she looked ready to leap.

Just as sudden as it had come, her mood shifted. Her head lowered from its haughty tilt and she looked wistful. "Small town area like this just keeps rotting from the inside and getting worse. Should have cut out of here some time ago. Nothing you can do but watch it get worse."

"You could help make it better," Poppy said.

Mary Ann ignored her. Her eyes were not fixed on

Poppy or Arthur, but on some vague point between them. "You know how I come to hook up with Donnie? Was at the gym and I was looking hot, but most of the men went out of their way to ignore me. Being with Steve did that. So, Donnie Angel is the only one looking at me, right through me it felt like. I go past and he says so low only I can hear, 'No one else will have you, will they? Same with me.' He was right, and he moved in. We'd have been fine if the money I'd been left was in trust, but I was liquid and the Dot-com investment craziness come along and Donnie just had to be a player. All we had went down in a swirl when that mess crashed. Hell, we could hardly keep the lights on here for a while. I had to connect with Steve, see if there was any way to get some money from him. Turns out, he said, there was."

A deep voice boomed from outside the bars. "You aren't telling tales out of school are you, baby?"

Mary Ann made the most dramatic shift Arthur had ever seen in an individual. One minute she was scrappy, confident. At the sound of the voice her head bowed, her shoulders slumped, and she made eye contact with none of them. She quivered like a dog expecting to be hit. That was probably the case.

Donnie opened the bars and came inside making the cell seem far smaller. He wore his hair slicked back with oil into a tight pompadour the same as it had been in high school. The touch of white in his sideburns did not detract from the impression that he had stayed far younger and fit than the rest of his class. He ignored Mary Ann for the moment and leaned down close so they could see his intense stare and wide fixed grin that did not bode well at all. It was like looking into the red flaming depths of hell and seeing Satan.

"I think you and I are going to have to have a chat, Poppy. You'll enjoy it. I'm pretty sure I know everything that's going on here, but I want to pry the details from you. No, you won't tell me at first, but we'll enjoy getting to the answers. Won't we?"

His head lifted up and away from them. The air around them felt ten degrees cooler. Pain throbbed up from Arthur's torso and settled in his head where it rang like a bell without a tongue.

"First Mary Ann and I have to go and discuss some discipline issues. Don't we, dear?"

"Please, Donnie. Oh, please." She could not help the quaver in her voice. It held the tune of raw fear.

Poppy nudged at Arthur's shoulder. He looked at her. She nudged again, harder.

Donnie leaned down again, grabbed Arthur's left ear and twisted it as hard as he could. It felt like it would tear all the way loose any second. "I'll want to have a few words with you too, but Poppy first. You can wait? Of course you can. Can't you?"

He stood and held Mary Ann's arm hard enough to bruise it while he escorted her out of the cell and clanged the door shut. He paused outside the bars. "Oh, and Poppy, cheer up. Remember, you'll always have Paris."

They could hear Mary Ann mewing and pleading as he tugged her down the stone hallway.

Poppy stood up and threw the wet cloth on the floor in

front of Arthur. "Tend to yourself." She paced to the far side of the cell and tried to look down the hallway through the bars.

"What?"

"That," she bit off the words, "was the biggest single act of cowardice I've ever witnessed."

"Who?"

"You."

"Are you . . .?"

"You still don't get it, do you? That man was abusing a woman right in front of you, and you just let him."

"What was I supposed to do?"

"You didn't even try. Have you ever heard that if you're not part of the solution then you're part of the problem?"

"How can you . . .?"

"Oh, just shut up and sulk with your little hurts. God knows what he's going to do to that woman, is maybe doing to her right now?"

Arthur could have said Donnie would probably be doing the same to Poppy all too soon. He kept his mouth shut. He could think of no win direction in sight. Hadn't he gone out to the plant just to impress her? He felt stupid, and as riddled by pain as he had ever been. Blood on his face was drying and any attempt at expression hurt. The stone wall behind him was cold and seemed to suck all the heat from him. His body began to shiver, even though he willed it not to.

Chapter Twenty Three

His cell phone rang and Dennis popped it open. Tricky to do with one hand keeping a gun pointed at Frankie's middle. He had to steer with his knees for a moment. He managed that and a sharp turn on the back road as well. "How's it going?"

"Depends on who you'd ask," Huff answered. "There's some good, but there's bad too."

"Oh?"

"Arthur and Wally went missing."

"We expected that, didn't we?"

"Yeah, but when Donnie showed up he only had Arthur with him."

"You think Wally was the leak in the balloon Arthur expected."

"That's one possibility."

"What else?"

"Turns out I don't need a lot of that surveillance stuff I lugged here, including some I made the drive to get."

"How so?"

"Place has a complete sound and video system already installed, for security. All I had to do was tap into that. I'm ready for transmission."

"How much time have we got?"

"Not much. Rod's ready to slow them down, but not too much. You're going to have to step lively or there will be hitches."

"Arthur allowed for some."

"Not as many as we might get, or already got. I don't like thinking of Wally as just a hitch."

"Maybe Wally's fine but just took a hiatus to slip off and see that girlfriend of his."

"If that's the case, he picked a helluva time for it."

Dennis snapped the phone shut and slid it back in his pocket. As they rounded the corner the lights lit up the parked vehicle ahead.

"What the hell?" Frankie had been silent on the ride until now.

Dennis pulled his truck up beside Huff's Lotus Cortina and turned off the engine. The car's trunk was open and empty.

"I suppose you aren't going to tell me what's going on here."

"Well, Frankie. You and I get to act as a sort of rear guard. We are going to slow Steve and Rolly down until your Bu friends wake up. That sound okay with you? If not, I can handcuff you and leave you here at the truck."

"I'll go. Why didn't you consult me on any of this?"

"I think you know the answer to that if you dig down deep enough." Dennis glanced down at his watch. "Let's wait here for a minute or two before we head on in. Give Steve and Rolly a chance to think everything's going fine. Okay? Timing's important."

"Where're the others? Out on a goose chases too?"

"Huff's done and in place. That leaves Rod. He's got his chores to do and then he'll be along as well."

"You didn't mention Wally."

"I guess I didn't."

Frank sat in silence, occasionally glancing to Dennis' hand that still held a gun, casual, but ready for use.

"That Steve is some piece of work, wouldn't you say?" Dennis said, after a few minutes had ticked by.

"How's that?"

"Look at the women all still tangled up in his life. Astrid heads up a Venezuelan cell trying to steal the uranium. The people of Venezuela have little reason to be fond of America just now, and you as well as anyone would know why. You were down there with the CIA doing some pretty nasty work. But Astrid had a special desire to kick sand in Steve's face. Mary Ann is on hand as the "go to" girl, an outlet when the heat cranked up. I don't believe any of your team saw that coming. And Poppy, you sure strung her along quite nicely."

"That how you see it?"

"You've been on Benton's hook all along. He has something on you. When he says jump you have to say, 'How high?' It was your job to make sure enough of the locals muddled up the mix so Steve thought he had to move the stuff. Well, you succeeded there."

"You sing pretty well with that roscoe in your hand."

"Oh, I respect you, Frankie. I'm fit, but you could take me. I know it. This is just to make you a better listener."

"I wish to hell you people would quit calling me Frankie."

"The thing that most bothers me is Benton. You carry some of his stink by association. I got on the force to protect and serve. I'm a peace officer, not a bully in uniform, and if anyone I'm responsible for gets hurt, I feel it. Benton doesn't care if there are a few casualties as long as he gets the headlines he's after, and he's got that tomfool Bob Kennedy singing in the choir with him."

"You figure out all this on your own?"

"Oh, I don't get any credit for that. Arthur figured it out. But I *am* enjoying it."

"How's this supposed to play out?"

"Well, Benton wants Steve to come out squeaky clean, for the centrifuge operation to move forward and hopefully rejuvenate a pretty screwed up uranium enrichment process. He'd like someone else to take the fall, preferably a nasty foreign power. He's got Astrid for that now, but no smoking gun to put in her hands. Me, I like Steve for the villain, possibly because that's the truth, however outdated that concept is to federal agencies used to manipulating the truth."

"You're starting to sound like Huff."

Dennis ignored him. "You see, Steve is a desperate man playing a desperate game. Like a lot of people who got very rich fast, and clawed their way getting there, he's not comfortable just sitting on that and easing toward a cushy retirement, unlike the rest of us who are likely to end up sitting around in rest homes in dirty underwear. Steve's thrill is the high wire, and he's stretched himself incredibly thin this time—doesn't need the money but loves the thrill of the chase, especially if he thinks he's beating it. The fancy footwork and misdirection, that's all his style. But you know all about that, don't you?"

"If you're done preaching, why don't we do something?"

Dennis looked at his watch. "You're right. It's time to get busy."

They stepped outside the truck. The moon wrestled with clouds and lost. The night grew almost black. Wind moaned through the trees, through which they could see the turrets of the castle rise far taller than either could have imagined.

Frankie could have taken off in a run, but Dennis figured he would stay and ride this out now. Benton was out there thrashing around and Frankie might still be able to do what he'd been asked to do.

"Yeah, it's my first time this close to the damned place myself," Dennis said, "and I can't say I'm all that thrilled about it." He moved spare clips for his gun into his jacket pocket where they would be easy to get to.

"Well, let's get this over with," Frankie sighed.

"We'd better take along the spike strips. We're going to need them."

They moved off through the trees into the dark of the night.

Chapter Twenty Four

Arthur could feel his open cuts and abrasions drying into scabs that cracked open each time he turned. The sharp stabs of two, maybe three cracked ribs shot through him like white jolts of lightning, and something internal felt ruptured and oozed and sloshed with each body shift he made. Worse, the cold wet rock of the floor seemed to pull every bit of warmth from his body, and the steady shiver and chill intensified each ache and pain. No wait. What was far worse was Poppy huddled over there on the far side of the cell. She might treat a leper with more kindness and warmth.

"Did you ever wonder how a castle came to be out in the middle of bumfart nowhere?"

"You don't need to entertain me. I've had quite enough of you for the moment."

"Well, Poppy, I tell stories. It's what I do. Plus I researched this for something a long time ago and never got to use it. It'll give me something to do."

"If we had the pot for it, you could boil your head for all I care." Poppy stayed huddled against the stone wall on the far side of the cell. Arthur's shivers accelerated until they rippled through him in waves, with increasing accompanying aches and an occasional sharp stab that made him twitch. He waited until he had enough control to keep his voice from wavering or jerking, and he talked to take his mind as far from the variety of pains as possible.

"When Martin Q. Reznick first approached the Plumber family about their Ohio property," Arthur said, "Jeremy Plumber figured the man was after the tourist trade. He had heard of Reznick and named a price he figured would give him leverage when they began to dicker. Instead, Reznick had reached for his checkbook and Mont Blanc fountain pen."

"Plumber's first reaction was to kick himself for not asking more, but by the time he held out a trembling hand for the check to blow on the ink to dry it he was already doing a mental jump and heel click that he would no longer be escorting screaming children and their bored parents into the earth to see Fairy Wing Falls, little more than a mud glissade he had helped along with its design, the Devil's Teeth stalactites, the Dwarf Stool stalagmites, or the Crystal Chieftain, the result of his father's satiric ingenuity. In the early nineteen-forties Hiram Plumber, an electrical engineer, speculated on quartz crystal after reading trade journal articles that suggested they might be useful for building electrical circuits. What he had not counted on was that they were so damned plentiful that any tomfool could buy a ton of them, as he had done. Stuck with the sparkling pile of stone, and having found the small entrance of a cave behind some bushes on his Ohio sixty-six acres of property sandwiched as it was between a rippled line of hills and Turtle Run Creek where no one in living memory had ever seen a single turtle, Hiram thought like an engineer and hauled the crystal underground where he glued it to a limestone cave wall in the rough shape of an Indian Chieftain's head. He hinted to the first tour that he ever guided into the cave that the mosaic had either grown that way or had been carved by an earlier civilization, a story he stuck with until a school teacher from Findlay, Ohio pointed out that the silhouette was that of a Sioux Chieftain, common on the great plains of the United State but not found too commonly in Ohio."

"Still and all, Chieftain Cavern remained a tourist attraction listed in almost every state guide and it drew a steady stream of visitors except for two weeks in the nineteen-sixties when epoxy hit the stores as a hot new affordable glue and Jeremy closed the cave to reattach loose parts of the chief and fill in gaps where children and a few adults had, against strict instructions, pried loose a sample."

"Jeremy was as surprised as everyone else when Reznick closed off the property from the public and instead of reaping the slowing but still steady stream of tourist dollars, instead began building a castle patterned after the same model Walt Disney had drawn from, the Neuschwanstein castle in Bavaria. The cave, on the castle grounds, he closed with a wrought iron gate and no one from the public ever entered it again. As the white towers rose up over the green trees, more than a few people passing by asked, 'What the hell?' After the construction crew finished with the moat and drawbridge they diverted their efforts to a stone wall with broken glass embedded on top along the road side of the estate and then completely around the rest of the grounds."

"The castle, as I came to understand it, realized a promise Martin had made to Mary Ann's mother, Minnie. Having lived up to the promise, he went back to his various mining interests, which meant he was often gone from the castle. Instead of flowering in the setting, Minnie withered and turned sour until two years after Mary Ann graduated from high school she died. The doctor said it had been her heart, but Mary Ann was never really sure her mother had one anymore."

"It was in this prison-like setting that Mary Ann Reznick grew up as princess in residence, I understand. She often stood in a tower and looked off toward the lights of Pikeburg and in the other direction at the nuclear plant. As far as anyone knew, Steve Hamilton was the only one who ever dared brave the castle to call on Mary Ann, and as often as not he picked her up at the gate, when he could."

Arthur thought he heard Poppy stir for a second when he mentioned Steve Hamilton, but she said nothing.

"The way I heard it, when Steve and she parted ways, Mary Ann came back to the castle where she was alone. Her father died, and the trust fund kept the place going. She waited a long time looking out from the tower until Donnie Angel came along. She apparently thought he had a nice, smooth way of saying hello to a girl so that it came across as if asking if she was wearing underwear. He was no prince, but then he had been no frog either."

He listened to the cold drip of water in the quiet for at

least a minute.

"You know, she said at last, with cold deliberation that made him try to sit up and made him just as sorry for trying, "if I were you I'd have picked almost any other fucking story in the world to tell other than that one."

Chapter Twenty Five

Water continued to drip down a stone wall far from their cell. Each drop now sounded like a bowling ball dropping to Arthur. His head throbbed and every effort to move was like shoving knives into his abdomen.

Poppy kept to her side, leaning against the stone wall as far from him as she could get. Anything Arthur had felt like a schoolboy crush had flittered away like some crippled cave bat. He thought he heard screams once, but that could have been him. As hard as he listened he could only hear distant whimpering moans and not the step of shoes on the stone hallway.

"Did you miss me?" Donnie stood outside the bars, turning the key in the lock. He wore his wide grin, which did nothing to calm Arthur. Though she prided herself in her independence and willingness to take crap from no one, Poppy took a step back as Donnie entered the cell. *Damn he was a tall lean one.*

"You'll have to forgive me. In a place this big the help can get unruly without a firm hand. Now, where were we?" His eyes were wide and intense, and he never blinked.

"You are an evil, evil man, Donnie, and you should be put down like a rabid dog."

"Well, I'm glad you're feeling chatty, Poppy, because

it's time you and I had a little talk, perhaps some unwilling sex to go along with that. Now, doesn't that sound like a bit of fun?"

"I'll bite you and kick you and claw you until I die."

"Oh, I think you'll find I have ways around all that. After a while, I think you're going to start to enjoy yourself. You have the sort of disposition that lends itself to that, with the proper application, and, baby, I'm damned good at application. You could say the best."

Arthur's eyes squeezed shut as he pushed himself off the floor and slid along the stone wall until he was standing upright. "She doesn't know anything," he said. "It makes no sense to even waste time working her over."

"Go on. I'm listening."

"Don't. He's an idiot."

"Poppy, let the man make his point. I'll decide."

"Think about it. Steve's had her tucked away and now you've been sitting on her. She knows *nothing* about what's going on. She's a waste of your time."

"It's too late to be gallant, Arthur. Give it up."

"Poppy, just shut the hell up. Will you? Everything isn't always about you."

"Oh, I like your touch with the ladies, Arthur. You could fit in around here. And you do probably know more than she does. Okay. You've sold me. I start on you, but I don't expect that to last too long. Do you? Then I'm coming back for Poppy, and that should be a whole lot more fun."

Donnie grabbed Arthur's wrist and tucked it up behind his back in a come along hold and headed for the cell door.

"Wait. No. Take me." Poppy rushed at them and the back of Donnie's hand clipped across the face with a sharp crack. She spun, crumpled to the floor, and lay there still.

"Did you kill her?"

"No, my little hero. She'll be fine. Better than you, really. I'll be back for her." Donnie moved them through the door and banged the cell door shut with a clang.

Arthur tried to look back, caught only a quick glance. She still had not moved.

*   *   *

"You think that will do it for now?"

"We did what we had to do, Rolly." Steve slid into the passenger seat and closed the door. Rolly started the engine and flipped on the lights. Steve glanced back. With the beams and warning signs back in place it didn't look like the cave entrance had been used in years. Perfect.

"I still think we should have had some of the men do this."

"We're stretched pretty thin. You've lost quite a few of your untouchable elite. Besides, it's best only we know."

The road swung around the base of the castle and out to the drawbridge, which they had left down. Thirty feet from the bridge the truck lurched and the front bumper sank slowly down until it plowed into the gravel and dirt and they stopped.

"What the hell?" Steve reached for the glove box and

Rolly already had a gun in his hand.

Spotlights clicked on and bathed the courtyard in white. Steve blinked.

"Toss them out the windows. You're both in the crosshairs." The loudspeaker voice came from the castle's system, but that wasn't Donnie or Mary Ann.

Rolly tossed his .9mm Glock out first. Steve pitched the P226 X-five tactical Sig Sauer he held out onto the gravel. He flinched as he heard it scrape on the rocks. He had spent a lot of rounds through that gun on his private range and he had hoped to be able to call on it when the time came.

"Step out of the vehicle, hands on your heads, and walk this way."

They stepped into the harsh lights and walked forward until they were told to stop. They heard the drawbridge begin to lift. As their eyes adjusted to the lights Steve could see the bridge lifting. From out of the shadows on either side stepped Dennis McBride and Frankie Lane. Dennis was not in uniform, but both men held guns pointed their way.

"It's not quite the same as having an unlimited supply of men to throw at a situation and clean up afterward, is it?" Dennis said.

"Now, Frankie, you know better than this," Steve said. "And Dennis, when Bob hears about this you're pretty much finished, no matter how all of this comes down."

"You mistake me for someone who gives a damn," Dennis said. "I'm not in this for the county. I'm in it for the country."

Rolly glanced his way and he understood. They

dropped their hands and ran toward Frankie and Dennis. Steve knew Dennis was a peace officer at heart, and Frankie no doubt had orders not to do anything to Steve. It was a good gamble, and it paid. No shots were fired.

Steve had played football and knew what to do. He lowered his head and dove toward Dennis, who stepped to the side, chopped him across the neck with his gun barrel, and had the gun tucked away before Steve could roll and twist upright to face him. Looked like Dennis had learned a thing or two at academy.

Dennis waited while Steve came in slow this time. From the corner of his eye Steve saw Frankie and Rolly going at it. Frankie gave up a few inches in height and reach, but he'd had some training and experience. Rolly was picking himself up and brushing off gravel. Steve returned his full focus to Dennis just in time to block a right cross. A kick to the side of his knee seemed to come from nowhere and he dropped one knee in the gravel and scrambled to get out of the way as Dennis surged closer.

He hadn't counted on this. Only a few seconds into feinting and punching, dodging some blows and catching a few others, Steve realized he was over his head with Dennis, who methodically picked apart Steve's offense and counter-punched as if he meant it.

The drawbridge was still rising. Rolly had backed halfway up it, trying to stay away from Frankie's kicks. One of his eyes was swollen half shut. This was not going well at all.

The first time Dennis took a peek to see how the other

two were doing Steve shot around him and ran for the open stone doorway beside the drawbridge. A spiral stone staircase circled its way upward and he raced along the steps, hearing Dennis close behind him.

The top of the stairs opened into a parapet walk surrounded by waist high notched battlements. He looked for anything he could use for a weapon. The steel handrail up the inside of the stairwell was bolted to the stone wall. Everything else was stone. He saw Rolly at the top of the drawbridge, which was three-quarters of the way up. The pitch looked quite steep, but Frankie fought his way to the top until the two of them were poised on the top of the closing bridge throwing punches and kicks so fast Steve could barely see them.

He spun and Dennis had squared off, blocking the way down. Steve knew that if he ran Dennis might be able to catch him, tackle him. "Look, maybe I went about it wrong. There must be things you need, or want, and I have a great deal of money, Dennis. Tell me what it will take."

"Speak into the camera, Steve, and smile. Nothing's being missed."

As soon as he looked up, saw the lens on the wall behind him, he felt Dennis twist his arm and heard the click of a handcuff and felt it tighten around his wrist. He gave a tug. The other end was fastened to the steel railing.

"I'm coming, Frankie." Dennis ran down the stairwell. He would be cutting it close. The drawbridge was almost to the stone wall above the arch.

Frankie and Rolly balanced with one foot on each angle. Rolly kicked and Frankie countered. Rolly fell and grabbed the top of the bridge with both arms. Frankie tottered and fell the other way, down toward the moat.

The bridge slammed shut with a bang. Rolly's arms and head hung for a moment then fell toward the water. Steve looked away.

Dennis ran back up the stairwell, panting. "Did they . . .? Did they . . .?"

There were rings in the water where Frankie had splashed in, smaller ones where what was left of Rolly had fallen.

"He's dead. You've killed him."

"Who? Rolly, or Frankie?"

"Rolly." Steve's voice broke. He surprised himself. He had never cried or even gotten choked up when he had separated from Poppy, Mary Ann or Astrid. This was different. Rolly had been his protector and friend for nearly fifty years.

Dennis stared down at the water. "Do you see anything?"

Steve looked. Nothing. He had not seen Frankie come out anywhere.

*   *   *

The first of the two vans, matching black GMC Suburbans, slumped to the pavement and scraped bumper for a dozen feet before grinding to a halt. Gerald Benton, riding shotgun in the front seat, was thrown forward and reached out to stop forward momentum just as his seat belt slammed into his collarbone. He swiveled to look at the driver, Dick Burroughs, who frowned and shrugged at the same time he undid his seatbelt and reached for the door handle. The van following behind started out around them.

"Tell them to stop," Benton yelled.

"Too late," Burroughs said as the second van's front sunk to the road.

They poured out of the vehicles with the others and looked at the four punctured tires.

"Get on those. Pronto," Benton shouted.

Burroughs had stepped off to the side of the road, away from the others.

"Just get one of them able to move," Benton shouted. "We'll have to leave a couple men behind with it. Parker and Williams, you two will stay." He wasn't going to have another Jacksonville, where an FBI van had been stolen, twelve weapons with it. The van was recovered as a burned out shell and they'd been two weeks tracking down the weapons, which included four sniper rifles, along with eighty rounds of .308 ammo. They never did recover a missing M-79 grenade launcher.

"Put that cell phone away, Burroughs. Who're you going to call? Triple-damn-A?" He had turned his own cell off when they had sent half the men off with the Venezuelans and the sheriff's crew.

"I was just . . ."

Burroughs, a seven-year man, transferred out of the East Coast seeking to make a name for himself, had gone to Brown and had an irritating habit of bringing up the Ivy

League too often. All Benton, who had gone to the University of Michigan, had to do was bring up football. That usually shut him up.

Benton stepped close. "Why don't you help the others? This could go faster."

The driver put the phone away and looked like he wanted to say something but thought better.

"This tells us two things," Benton said. "We're headed in the right direction, and someone doesn't want us to come this way. That someone is interfering with a federal investigation and I'm going to personally see that they're mighty damn sorry before this is over."

*   *   *

Dennis stared down at the water.

"How about you loosen this handcuff? It's pinching me," Steve said.

"No."

A single headlight came up the road. A motorcycle swept around the bend and pulled up on the other side of the moat.

"Rod, that you?" Dennis yelled down. "How much time do we have?"

"About ten minutes, maybe less if they figure out to put the good wheels from the other vehicle on just one of them and keep coming. Open the drawbridge."

"What can it hurt?" Dennis muttered and started back down the stairs.

Steve tugged at the handcuff holding him to the rail. Nothing doing. He did look away when he heard the drawbridge being lowered with what was left of Rolly on it.

Chapter Twenty Six

Time ticked by slowly in the dank stone cell. Then the key turned in the lock and Poppy looked up to see Donnie carrying something over his shoulder. This was the first time she had seen him not grin. The eyes were just as intense as ever. He looked serious, and mad. That was not good at all.

The door opened and he tossed Arthur onto the floor. Arthur groaned, so at least he was not dead. He rolled onto his side and spit out a tooth. A small puddle of blood came with it.

"Now, sweetheart. I believe it's your turn. I got nothing from him." He spit down onto Arthur, who did not move or flinch.

Arthur's lips moved, though. "She knows nothing," he mumbled.

Donnie kicked him hard.

Arthur doubled and she heard bubbling sounds as he sucked air.

"You just wasted my time, and I don't have all that much," Donnie said.

"Running out," Arthur mumbled.

Donnie drew his foot back.

"Stop. Please."

Donnie held up a hand. "Shut up, bitch. Listen."

She heard only a faint rumble.

"Someone's messing with the drawbridge. I'll be back, and you won't like it, won't like it a bit." This time he managed a grin, but it was in no way an encouraging one.

He spun and was out the door with the cell door banging behind him.

Poppy stooped down beside Arthur, drew the bucket of water closer and tore a piece off her own shirt this time.

"I was so wrong about you Arthur. I'm so sorry. I know you may not even be able to hear me. If you can, stay awake and hang in there. I was . . .I was just off balance, seeing Mary Ann after all these years. It's all been about Steve in my head. I felt so stupid, and guilty about cheating on Pecky, a kind man with a heart as big as the capital building who certainly didn't deserve anything like the life I made for him in his last years. I've been wrong, about a lot of things, and especially people. Just hold on, Arthur. Please."

*　　*　　*

The wind tugged at the camouflage tarp and Huff reached up to tighten the rope that looped around the base of a sycamore tree. He had seen no one patrolling the grounds, but Arthur has said there would be at least one moment when things could start to slip and go in a wrong direction. He didn't want it to be because of anything he did or didn't do. The rows of dials glowed as they picked up and recorded the sounds from all mikes. He switched from camera to camera on the row of three laptops in front of him. Tapping into the system had taken him about five minutes longer than he had expected to configure his system to that of the castle security setup. Once he was getting live feed he flipped through the various cameras until he saw Poppy in her dungeon cell. The cell door opened and Donnie dropped Arthur to the stone floor like a bag of wet sand. Sure didn't look like Arthur was having a very good day. Poppy tended to Arthur's cuts and bruises as Huff set up the live feed so all he would have to do is type in a command and the whole thing would be streaming. He checked and double-checked the transmission numbers. Some of it was busy work to keep him from having to look at the two of them in the dungeon cell. When Arthur had given Huff and Dennis the complete briefing before talking to the others he had said there were going to be some moments where it would be tough to wait, but that it is imperative they do just that, no matter what, so that the timing is exact.

Done with all the fiddling he could do before admitting he was as ready as he was ever going to be, Huff turned up the sound and adjusted his headset. It wouldn't do to miss any mushy chatter down there, although it sounded far from high romance so far. He watched while Mary Ann came into their cell and the conversation took a soap opera turn. He caught himself glancing at his watch as much as he watched their screen. He flipped through the other cameras, keeping an eye on the courtyard, but was drawn back to the dungeon cell just in time to see Donnie Angel enter and drag Mary Ann away.

The courtyard got busy when Frankie and Dennis arrived in time to stop Steve and Rolly from leaving. The fighting there had Huff glued to two screens that picked up as much as he could see there. He flipped around the other security cameras until he found the cell where Donnie and Mary Ann were the central figures. He gasped, flipped away only to reluctantly flip back. He couldn't take his eyes away. Part of him wanted to call 911, whatever. He had never been married himself, but had heard of spouse abuse. But he had never even imagined anything like this. Donnie seemed to favor combinations of punches and electric chock. Bending close to whisper questions. He was being good cop and bad cop at the same time, although the kindness of his whispered questions was a mockery Huff could see through and knew Mary Ann did as well. Huff finally had to turn off the sound. He could no longer take her screams. He reached up to his face, surprised to find it wet. He could not remember the last time he had cried, yet his cheeks were covered in tears.

In one of the castle courtyard cameras he watched Dennis handcuff Steve to a railing. He glanced to the other screen in time to see Frankie fall from the top of the drawbridge. He gasped and flipped through all the camera setting he could find until he got a shot of the moat. Nothing.

He began to think he had the hardest job of all. Watching it all happen and not being able to do a damned thing.

Back in the torture cell Donnie was almost tender as he took Mary Ann down from the stone wall. He murmured to her as he carried her away. Sweet nothings, Huff supposed as he checked on the courtyard again. He had to hop back through the cameras until he got to the dungeon cell in time to hear Arthur argue his way into being taken first. Silly fellow. If he could have seen what Mary Ann just endured Huff doubted he could have managed. The way Donnie clubbed Poppy to the floor as he led Arthur away should have hinted at what to expect.

Now the waiting was worse. Huff found himself liking Arthur more than he had. The notion had been growing, but he had never expected Arthur to let himself in for anything like this just to save Poppy. For a reason he couldn't explain, he recalled the scenario after Gary Hart, then a frontrunner presidential candidate, was caught having an extramarital affair with Donna Rice. Followers said it was like a Greek tragedy. Huff disagreed. The true element missing from that being a "tragedy" was any noble intention. He could find nothing like it in anything Hart had done. But Arthur here had gone into this with his eyes open. This got uglier by the moment.

At first he couldn't watch. Then he was drawn to the screen, mesmerized. This was far worse than Donnie had been with Mary Ann. There was none of the alternating kindness that probably was more salt in the wound than real. This was raw meanness of a kind Huff had never imagined possible, even as he kept up on the Edi Amins and Ayatollah Khomeinis of the world, and this was in his own back yard, a product of the same school they'd all attended.

He realized that he was shaking and his face was covered with tears again. He had his cell phone in hand and was dialing. To hell with this whole thing. He had to get Arthur out of there.

Donnie stepped back and Huff got a good look at Arthur, who lifted his head and looked right at the camera. It seemed to take everything he had, but he said out loud, "Wait. Wait until the time is . . ."

"What the hell're you talking about?" Donnie said. He stepped in close and picked up the intensity of the beating.

It took everything Huff had to close his cell phone and slip it back in his pocket. He flipped through every camera the castles security system had, to ensure there would be no more surprises. He saw Rod come across the drawbridge on his bike. When he flipped back to the dungeon cells Arthur was back on the stone floor and Poppy bent over him. Donnie had gone. Huff flipped frantically through the cameras until he caught a glimpse of Donnie running up stone stairs with a bolt cutter clenched in one hand. He must have seen Steve handcuffed to that rail.

Huff grabbed for his phone and hit the speed dial. Dennis picked up. Before he could speak, Huff shouted, "Guys, the bull is loose in the China shop." He hung up, hoped he had been in time.

*   *   *

225

Donnie burst out into the courtyard, talking long deliberate strides toward them, not running, but not strolling either. Such was his self-confidence that he hadn't even bothered to bring a gun, just held a bolt cutter in one hand. His other hand clenched and unclenched into a fist and his always intense eyes had gone up a level into an eager glare.

Dennis reached around his back for his gun, but Rod climbed off the motorcycle. "Don't waste a bullet on him."

The two did not hesitate. Donnie stood as tall as Rod, but gave away a few pounds. He took deliberate steps until he was close enough to swing the bolt cutters as hard as he could right at the knee they all knew had cost Rod his football career. Rod faked a hip and dodged in the other direction. Donnie threw the cutters at Rod's head. He ducked. The cutters flew past and Rod rushed toward Donnie without missing a step. The two of them smashed together like two mountain sheep butting heads. Donnie came in swinging, but the blows bounced off Rod. Dennis could hear the loud crunch of bone, though, and was pretty sure Rod's nose got broke in the first couple of punches, but he never slowed. He waded in and grabbed Donnie Angel by the chest and lifted. Donnie had cold, hard experience. But Rod was fueled by all the emotional rage that had built up by not being able to do anything about Paul's death, and now Wally's.

Donnie swung as hard as he could, his fists smashing into Rod's neck and the back of his head hard enough to fell any other two men. Donnie's punches came quicker, and harder. Desperate now. Rod was taking a terrible beating without being able to punch back. Dennis wished he had just put Donnie down, shot him like a mad dog, even if that went against every bit of academy training he'd had. Rod arched his back and squeezed. In high school he had been able to bench press five hundred pounds and Dennis did not figure he had lost much of that. Donnie's blows grew even more desperate and wild. Dennis heard the loud crack and Donnie's arms stopped and he slumped like a rag doll across Rod's shoulders.

Rod shrugged the body off and let it fall to the courtyard. "The man packed a punch. I'll say that." He started to laugh, hard enough to bend him at the waist before he straightened again. He rubbed a knuckle at the corner of his eye.

Dennis stared at him. "What?"

"I was just thinking that if Donnie has a ghost it's going to be upset he got hugged to death by a gay man." Rod reached a hand up to his face to swipe at the blood pouring from his nose.

"Let's get the others and get out of here. Okay?" Dennis took out a pocket handkerchief and handed it to Rod. They broke into a run.

*   *   *

The black van pulled across the drawbridge, eased around what was left of Rolly, a torso and shattered legs, went out around the white pickup with two front flat tires, and stopped short of Donnie Angel's lanky corpse.

Men in black flak jackets poured out of the back side doors and spread out. Gerald Benton climbed out of the passenger side and looked around. There was no sign of Frankie or the others.

"Up here."

He looked to the stairwell. That was Steve's voice. His men started that way. "You clear the rest of the area. I'll take this alone."

They knew procedure and hesitated. "Do what I said," he snapped.

At the top of the stairs, bathed in the lights, Steve tugged at the handcuffs that held him to the rail.

"Just a minute." Benton fished for his keys and got the handcuff key. He opened the end holding Steve's wrist. "You're not supposed to be here. Where's Rolly?"

Steve rubbed his wrist. "He's dead. That's what's left of him down there by the bridge."

"Well, get out, and make sure you take what's left of Rolly with you. *Now.*"

"Will you shut up."

"Get out now. I'll clean this up."

Steve grabbed Benton's suit sleeve and spun him. He pointed up to the camera.

"We'll take care of that," Benton said.

"I don't think so." Dennis McBride stepped around the corner. He had changed into his uniform. "Someone went over your head, Benton, and tipped off Homeland Security.

Everything that's happened here in the past few hours and right to this minute has been piped in a direct feed to them. I just heard from them and they'll be here any minute. Your boss's boss didn't sound too pleased about being awakened at this hour and shuffled off this way in a jet. Smart of you to turn off your cell phone or he'd be chewing your ear off now. Turns out you're supposed to keep him in the loop on things like weapons grade uranium going missing. Who knew?"

"Stand down, deputy. You're interfering in a federal investigation."

"I don't think so. The guys seeing and hearing everything that's happened here, and is happening even as we speak, may see it differently." Huff's being able to tap directly into the castle's existing security system had sure made everything easier.

Gerald started to raise the service piece he held in one hand.

"Don't shoot the messenger," Dennis cautioned. "Remember, this is all on tape."

*   *   *

The motorcycle, going as fast as it could, faded until its headlight was dim and then gone. Huff glanced into the mirror past Poppy's head. Nothing was behind them. He shifted and gave the Lotus more gas. The car could flat out go, but it gave him no joy at the moment.

"How's he holding up?"

"Just get us to the hospital. He's not bleeding on your seats back here. His head's on my lap, if that's what you were worried about."

Huff didn't respond.

"You should have seen him back there. Why did he do that?" she said.

"Arthur told us everything to expect, even the twists and turns, although we couldn't know about Wally, just knew that someone would turn rat. Myself, I thought it would be Frankie. The point is, Arthur knew there was only one way to get to you and rescue you, and he expected to take some lumps to accomplish that."

"Well," she choked, "he sure as hell did that."

"Dennis said Frankie fell into the moat and didn't come out. What do you make of that?"

"That a lot of people were hurt or killed here. I hope some good came from it."

"How're you holding up?"

"I'm fine," but there was a deeper catch in her voice. "Just get Arthur to the hospital. Okay?"

Chapter Twenty Seven

The sheriff's department cruiser came up the lane, slow and cautious, just like before at Huff's place. It stopped a ways from the piles of timber and parked trucks of the construction workers. The door opened and Dennis McBride stepped out. His badge glittered gold when a ray of sunlight caught it. He sauntered over to where Arthur sat in a cedar Adirondack chair with a stemmed glass of red wine on one arm. Arthur's chest was still wrapped in a brace and he had one leg propped up on a wooden box. Most of the tape had been removed from his head by now, but he would wear a few scars for life, and he needed to see a dentist soon.

"Kind of early to be having a libation, isn't it?" Dennis said.

A big man on a ladder waved at Dennis and he waved back.

"Doctor says it helps me relax. Being around Rod's crew has me all a jangle."

"You sure look it. Turns out, I see, Rod is good at this sort of work."

"I'll bet he's going to be even better when it comes to the interior design."

"What do you mean by that?"

"Oh, nothing. I was being a smart mouth there for a second. You've got to give him and Bitsy credit. They're both still mourning Paul and Wally but have decided to forgive the past and grow old together gracefully. I think it's been working for them, so far."

"So I hear. I've been too busy with a town full of media vans from every broadcast station I've heard of and a few I haven't. Journalists still fill every motel room, right up to the broom closets. And, since the uranium enrichment plant is a no-fly zone, every gazoony with a helicopter has been flying around the castle taking footage for that 'film at eleven.' Well, the story sure enough broke, didn't it?"

"Like a fifty pound watermelon being dropped from New York City's Chrysler building. I did like that line from the Homeland Security spokesperson when he said it was high time the CIA and FBI had worked so well together. 'Like a smoothly oiled machine.' You can't out-cliché government staff once they roll up their sleeves.

"Talk's around town that some movie big shot was overheard saying he liked the idea of Jennifer Lopez playing the part of Astrid Lazo. Maybe they can get someone like Jack Nicholson to play you, kind of demented and off-balance."

"They should get a clown from a circus to play me. I've just stuck to the script of the story the Homeland Security gave me: a man swept along by circumstances bigger than himself. There's enough truth in that I had no trouble saying it. I'm lucky enough not to be in a cell somewhere."

"The others have all been hushed into the same story.

Maybe it's as well Frankie isn't around to tell his version. Who do you think'll get that part? Someone like Travolta?"

"I don't know. Sure was a swell picture in uniform of the young Franklin P. Lane they had in the paper. What was he? Twenty then?"

"About that. There are suddenly a lot of snappy stories about him. Some might even be close to true. I heard some cock-and-bull version where a major general from the pentagon was quoted in the *Washington Post* as saying there are a number of older, still active agents like Frankie, working across America and the world to keep everyone safe. I guess that notion is okay to buy as long as all across Ohio the hills fill in with green and the spring mushrooms quietly pop up on the musty slopes and in the low shadows of the woods, while people hike, fly kites, and wonder out loud, as they always do, if the corn is going to be 'knee high by the Fourth of July.'"

"You know Dennis, I had no idea you could wax so poetic. Maybe they should have had you give Frankie's eulogy."

"I'm a regular Henry Freaking Wadsworth Longfellow since they made me sheriff. I'll be kissing babies and giving speeches next. But I wouldn't have done Frankie much good at his memorial service here. I'd have laughed like a hyena."

Arthur shook his head, which fortunately, he thought, didn't rattle out loud. "I hear there's talk of renaming the Pikeburg High School building after him. In a service at Arlington National Cemetery every military branch was represented; shots were fired; and the Air Force flew the

233

missing wing formation over the ceremony. A *Columbus Dispatch* story said that at least a dozen new mothers had named their babies Frank."

The steady bang of a hammer drew Dennis' gaze back to the house. "Why're you building it even bigger than it was?"

"Oh, you never know. Might need room for grandkids someday."

"Aren't you a little long in the tooth to be starting a family?"

"I didn't say they'd necessarily be *my* grandkids." Before Dennis could respond, Arthur hit him with a change-up. "How's that new job suit you?"

"The usual horse shit politics. There were one or two of Bob's select men I might of kept, but they all got the ax when he did. Hell, I didn't ask the others to pick me to be acting sheriff until the next election. I doubt I run. I liked life better as a deputy."

"You'll run, and you'll win. A fellow like you in the center of a high profile case who has even shaken hands with the president. Your public calls."

"Well, I didn't get a handshake from the head of the FBI. He's still cleaning up Benton's egotistical mess. They didn't need that after 9/11."

"It's good to be small time, isn't it?"

"Yeah. Say, do you have another glass?"

"Sure." The wooden box his foot rested on held the rest of the set of Waterford glasses. By bending to one side he could get one out without taking his foot off the rest.

While Arthur poured him a glass, Dennis fumbled around and pulled a postcard out of his pocket. "You're gate's a mess, but the mailbox was still there. This was in it. Are you going to have the gate put back up again?"

"I don't believe I will this time. I need to stay more a part of the world." Arthur looked at the card. "Did you read this?"

"Yeah. Just nosy, I guess."

"What did you make of it?"

Dennis shrugged, but smiled. He raised a finger to scratch his streaked eyebrow, then raised his glass and took a sip.

Arthur took another sip too and looked at the card again. It was from Costa Rica. In block letters, the message said: IF YOU WRITE IT, MAKE YOURSELF THE HERO. It was signed: F.

"Yeah, I'll be damned," Dennis said.

"There are a few who will be missed at the reunion. Huff and Poppy are still busy with that."

"Where's she now?"

"Probably over talking in French to that dog of hers."

"Lucky Rolly isn't the sure-shot he thought he was. Maybe she'll get that honeymoon in France someday."

"Maybe."

"Oh, yeah." Dennis reached into his jacket and pulled out a blue red and white envelope. "This was this in your mailbox too. Wouldn't happen to be a couple open-date tickets on Air France, would it?"

Arthur grinned to himself, and his face gave a twinge where it still had not recovered all the way.

"At least it won't be Steve taking her," Dennis said. "He's probably going to end up locked up good no matter how many lawyers he decides to hire since Benton decided to roll over on him to save his own skin. Although, I suspect if the agency keeps him Benton is going to find himself posted to some exotic site like, say, Bumfart, South Dakota. I suspect having Unitalon taken away from him stings Steve even more."

Arthur stayed quiet, content to let Dennis do most of the talking. He had wanted all his life to be a better listener and, by gum, he might just make it yet.

"Of course," Dennis said, "on my end, I've got to deal with all these Homeland Security dudes who have the plant under lockdown until everything's accounted for. At least they're straight shooters, even if they're no more chatty than the Great Wall of China. Looks like the EPA is stepping up its act too. They say the environment is a mess around here and they want it cleaned up. Something very good is going to come of all this, unless it's all chatter leading up to an election year. But I do believe we'll all be better off."

Arthur shared a smile and took a sip of wine. Dennis picked up the slack.

"I hear Mary Ann is selling the castle to pay legal fees, and that Huff might buy it. He must make a pile from his inventions. I guess you weren't the only one with a secret side."

"He should be able to put together a hell of a panic room in a castle, although I hope he doesn't expect a visit from me. I have some of the same bad memories Mary Ann must have. I don't know how Huff's going to replace all those files he'd collected when he lost his place."

"Yeah, well you lost your home too."

"You lose a little, you gain a little. Maybe it was enough to realize that the measure of passion is how much you will give up for a thing, even if you don't expect to get it."

"You've changed."

"How so?"

"Seems like you're more willing to share your life with others now. That go for Poppy too?"

"It does seem more possible."

"You going to put that in one of your books?"

"I don't think I'm ready to talk about it in print yet. Maybe someday."

"Come on. Tell. How's it going with you and Poppy?"

"You know how it is. I write fiction, so I have to be careful about the scenes and happy endings I paint in my head. Hollywood's got a lot to account for one of these days, and I haven't gotten to this crusty state of bachelorhood by helping grease that chute."

"But you have a lot of good history, even more now, don't you?"

"Oh, we fight and spar a bit."

"She's chasing you. That's her way. You kind of enjoy the arguing now, don't you?"

"I suppose there's a slim chance we could coexist in an approximate space and though we would probably argue and make each other half crazy most of the time we could snatch one or two moments of joy from the goop of life that whirls by."

"What do you plan to do about it?"

Arthur hesitated, looked off into the green canopy of leaves. All the trees had their full compliment by now.

"Let her chase. After a while I may just slow down a bit—and let her catch me."

ABOUT THE AUTHOR

Russ Hall lives in hill country of Texas on the north shore of Lake Travis.

Prior to spending his time writing, hiking, and fishing, he worked for more than twenty-five years as an editor for major publishing firms, ranging from Harper & Row to Simon & Schuster to Pearson.

He has had more than a dozen books published, including a series featuring Esbeth Walters and a previous collection of short stories featuring the Blue-Eyed Indian, which won the Nancy Pickard Mystery Fiction Award. Two hardbacks in the Blue-Eyed Indian series, *Bones of the Rain*, and *South Austin Vampire*, come out in 2010.